THE REIGN OF

SILENCE

HEAVY LIES THE CROWN

BY D. FISCHER

ISBN: 978-1-952112-54-6

To You.
May you become who you're truly meant to be.

Everything in this book is fictional. It is not based on true events, persons, or creatures that go bump in the night, no matter how much we wish it were...

Contents

CHAPTER ONE

The moon shines through a frosted window in Bastian's home, splashing across the wood planks and many furs that squat against the far wall of the dining space. Sibyl catches Bastian's eyes wandering to the moon, the stars, and then finally, the furs. She knows he's thinking about who would normally be there, sprawled across their soft and plush fibers: Nefari Ashcroft, Princess of the Shadow Kingdom, his young charge.

Queen, Sibyl corrects herself. *Queen Ashcroft,* for if she still denies her title by the end of this journey, she will be an ignorant fool, and they'll all be damned.

This evening, Swen Copsteel fills Fari's place, silent and watchful in that certain way the record keeper normally is. His lips are curved up, and his hands are folded across his rotund belly.

On the stand next to him, there's fresh and hot tea left forgotten entirely. Sibyl finds it unusual that the old man had forgotten about his steaming brew, but perhaps what is transpiring before his very eyes is far more entertaining than his evening of steeped mint and chamomile.

Or, perhaps what's more entertaining is the way Bastian blatantly dismisses. . . everything Sibyl has to offer him.

She's surrounded by fools, she realizes.

"Close your eyes again, Bastian," Sibyl barks. She's been sitting across from him at his table for an hour now, and she has better things to do if he's not going to participate. But her Wiccan tools are already spread out before them; a bowl of goat's blood from the latest sacrifice sits at her elbow, a pile of pebbles by her wrist, and scattered across the table are seashells and rodent bones, her new favorite trinkets after the display of magic during the Harvest Storm.

He snaps his gaze back to hers. Then, he turns his attention to the fate card and the skull of omens intermixed between her cherished possessions. His eyes narrow at the rodent bones with uncertainty as if, at any moment, the tiny jaws will reach out and bite him.

It isn't that he doesn't trust Sibyl; she knows he does. But her ways are foreign still to him, even after all these years. Her magic is raw and powerful and great, and anything out of his control is terrifying. Sibyl knows this, too.

She taps the table with a long, pointed fingernail. "Touch the skull, and close your eyes, or you will not get to see what knowledge your heart desires."

With a wrinkled nose and a snarling lip, he obeys. His fingers tentatively touch the aged skull, and when he closes his eyes, she utters, "Good, good. Now, search, Bastian. Search within."

Sibyl places her hand over his when he's quiet for several heartbeats, his breathing slow and labored. His eyes had been shifting behind his eyelids, and she wonders what he is seeing.

As soon as the chill of her hand seeps into the warmth of his, the skull gasps, and in Nefari's younger self's voice, the skull cries, "Run, Bastian! Run! Run!"

Images play in Sibyl's mind; a dash through the Shadled forest, thunderous hooves of a frantic centaur, and the sobs of a child on his back. The purple leaves are thick above them, blotting out the sun entirely, and a crone scuttles from branch to branch like a spider, chasing them.

"Run, Bastian, Run! Run!" Sibyl and the skull cry together.

The vision fully overtakes her, and her head tips to the ceiling while her eyes roll continuously.

She can feel the muscles in Bastian's legs scream for reprieve. He's galloping as fast as he can, leaping over

10

roots and avoiding the wide cracks in the thirsty Shadled dirt. Glowing Diabolus Beetles take flight in the clatter of their haste, and somewhere behind them, the soft cackle of the crone sounds through the dark forest. The sound sends shivers across Sibyl's skin. Shivers and anger and fear all at once.

The screams of the young version of Nefari and the now version collide.

An arrow whizzes past Bastian's head, and Sibyl's heart hammers at the near-miss. But the arrow wasn't for him. No. The arrow was for the crone who was soaring mid-leap, heading the other direction.

The vision ends when Bastian yanks his hand away from the skull of omens with a hiss. Sibyl blinks the room back into focus.

"That isn't what I wished to see," he growls, face scrunched in fury.

"Come now, Bastian," Swen chastises. "The young crone cannot choose what you see."

Sibyl grips the edge of the table and squints at the Rebel Legion leader. "The skull of omens does not lie. This is what your heart wanted to see."

"A memory? If I wanted a memory - this particular memory - I could recall it myself."

"Who says it's nothing more than a memory?" She smirks then relaxes on her stool. "Besides, the memory is not of the journey. It is what is behind it that matters."

He crosses his arms, folds his four legs underneath them, and lowers himself to the ground. This brings him eye-level with Sibyl and more comfortable for her aching neck. He can be an intimidating sight, but his height bothers her most.

"What do you mean?"

"You're worried, aren't you." It wasn't a question, but Bastian opens his mouth to answer anyway. The pieces of jewelry on her wrist clink against each other when she holds up a hand. "You're worried she won't return as the same girl you brought home ten years ago. As the same woman who left here."

His jaw flexes, rippling the skin along his cheek. "Yes."

Sibyl rolls her neck in a frustrated sort of way. "Well, isn't that boring? Bastian Pike, the fearless leader, is afraid his duckling will return all grown."

Swen chuckles under his breath.

"Do not mock me."

She leans forward, a child challenging a behemoth of a man. "The situation calls for it. You're being a fool. Of course, she won't return the same. Of course, this journey will change her. And isn't that what we all wanted?"

"She cannot be queen here," Swen adds.

Sibyl curtly nods. "She must find her footing on her own, and this journey - this mission to retrieve her mother's crown - *her* crown - will change her in ways we all should hope for."

He looks away and glares at the moon. "That's not it."

"Oh? Something more interesting, then?"

The table groans when he slams his fist onto it, but Sibyl doesn't jump. She's used to his emotions when they get the best of him. "I'm worried she won't return at all! I'm worried she'll get herself killed!"

A pregnant pause pulls the room into an awkward silence.

"And what of the others?" she presses. "Dao, Kaymen, Cyllian, Fawn, Patrix? The poor excuse for man, Emory? What of them?"

Swen sighs. "Dao will be fine. He has all the history this realm has to offer and, therefore, will always find a way."

Bastian sucks on a tooth. "Patrix can take care of himself if he manages to stay out of trouble long enough. And the others, Savage will take care of them if he knows what's good for him."

"Ah, the deal you struck," Sibyl remembers the leverage Bastian has over the old Pirate King well. Though Sibyl appears to be young, she has lived longer than her appearance suggests.

Many do not know of this. What had transpired between Bastian and Savage had occurred and become destructive just before Bastian saved Nefari and the others from the Shadow Kingdom. Bastian was in love, but not with any normal maiden. He had been charged with training Luxlynn Billihook, who was Nefari's current age at the time. Savage Deeds wanted his own daughter to be well-versed in sword and in hand-to-hand combat and had employed Bastian to teach her everything he knew.

But the teachings quickly turned into something of obsession and love, a dangerous combination.

When Savage found out about the relationship, he betrayed Bastian by filling his daughter full of lies. His daughter refused to see Bastian afterward, and when Bastian confronted Savage on the matter, Savage had said he didn't want his daughter to be associated with someone who saved villages and did not plunder them. He assured Bastian the relationship would be destructive, and he warned him to stay away from her.

This is what Bastian holds over the head of Savage Deeds - a betrayal worse than a sword in the back. This was a betrayal to the heart, and since Savage does not like to owe anyone favors, he will not refuse Bastian this

14

one request: Take Dao, Cyllian, Kaymen, and Fawn to Hope's Island so they may harvest the only thing that can save those from the Queen of Salix's dark magic.

Inferaze.

"He won't refuse me," Bastian murmurs. "Not if he knows what's good for him."

"And Nefari and the Salix Servant, Kristal?" Sibyl asks coyly. "Who shall protect them?"

He looks back to her now. "You. *You* will watch for them with your . . . tools." He peers at the table and its spelled contents. "You will tell me what I need to know when I need to know it. Do you understand, Sibyl?"

She chortles. "Do you think I'd let her go on this journey without my naked eye?"

"She will cleave the darkness," Swen whispers. "But her journey until then is up to her."

CHAPTER TWO

Evening mist floats past the shores of the thin river traveling through Calhoun, a village sandwiched between the Shadled, the Kadoka Mountains, and the Black Market. The wind passes through the small village's meager market, abandoned at this hour of the night.

The mist curls around Nefari's feet and teases her calves with a damp chill. The sun had dipped past the horizon an hour ago, and now the moon's brilliant beams make the mist brighten considerably like veils of white cloth.

Her boots are soundless against the dirt alleys that weave between the taverns, inns, and brothels. She had heard the signs of someone's muffled cry for help moments ago and again just now.

She moves faster, pommel gripped by her hand.

I will not stand in the shadow of my past, Nefari chants in her head, having grown accustomed to the words that

16

bring her comfort ever since she left the safety of the Kadoka Mountains without the Rebel Legion's protection.

I will not stand in the shadow of my past. I will not -

Another scream. She softly pulls her sword from its sheath, still chanting the words in her head.

The mist parts, ushering her through another alley and into the shadows of the inn. It's the inn she and the others are staying in, their horses stabled in the back. She can hear them knicker and whinny to the woman's desperate calls for help, sensing the danger that lurks in the quiet of the night.

There, just ahead, is a man with long, tangled hair. His hands are on the woman, roving and roaming to his own wicked intent. Another man is beside him, grinning as he pinches a coin from inside her purse and brings it to his nose. Behind them are two more, anxiously waiting in the light of their torches.

Nefari moves, crouching low and tucking herself tightly into the shadows, her sword a reassuring weight in her hand. Her black leather outfit provides her with the protection of being near invisible, and the shadows hugging her skin make her appear as nothing more than a dark wraith.

The thought sends a shiver crawling down her spine.

The man groping the woman doesn't see it coming. She thrusts her inferaze blade, and it slides through the man's back like butter.

For a split second, all is soundless. But then, the man finally gasps. With her sword where it is, it surely can't be comfortable to breathe.

The man's knees buckle as Nefari tugs her sword back, and then he falls like a sack of wheat.

She and the woman lock eyes. Nefari need not bark the order. Without fixing her dress's shoulder straps or her cloak's crookedness, the woman dashes down the path in the direction from which Nefari had come.

The other men pull their swords, nicked and poor excuses of steel.

"You're going to die, little girl," one proclaims. The other spits his agreement onto the ground, and the man with the pinched coin backs away, dropping the purse entirely.

The two chuck their torches to the ground and step closer with a menacing edge to their swagger. Her fear dissipates, replaced with the hunt - the game - the thrill.

Nefari grins, cracks her neck, and then wordlessly clashes swords with the one nearest her. The man with the coin darts from the alley, but she pays him little mind. She whirls and spins and dips and rises, a dance she had been worried she could no longer perform since the Harvest Storm.

Adrenaline rises within her, fueling her to move faster, swifter, and cunningly. With one last slash of her blade, the alley falls quiet.

It ended too quickly. Men like this should die horrible deaths.

The torches lick the dirt where they were thrown, the flames reflecting against her black leather as she blows out a breath to calm her adrenaline. Her shadow-shaded hair, spilled over her face, shines dully under the scrutiny of the moon.

She bends to the first who had died. "Well, aren't you a lucky bastard," she grumbles. "This could have been way more fun. For me, at least."

Using the man's tunic, she wipes her blade clean. When she stands, a tossed coin clinks against the path, rolls, then spins by her feet. She frowns at it and would have picked it up, but a short blade is pressed to the hollow of her throat, and her back is pressed to a hard chest.

She freezes.

Foul breath brushes against her cheek. "Move, and I'll split this pretty little neck."

"I -" she doesn't get to finish her threat. She sees a glint and moves her head to the side at the last second. A short knife embeds into the man's eye. He drops, and on the way down, his own knife knicks her skin. She hisses to the pain of it and covers the small wound with her palm.

"What in Divine's name," she curses, squinting in the direction from which the blade had come, the coin left entirely forgotten. All she sees is misty darkness.

The shadows bend toward her as the silence stretches on, but with a soft gale, the fog parts again. Where the alley spills out into the curved main road, a figure stands. She can't make out any features. There's a hood over the face, but she's sure this person is male with wide, broad shoulders and at a height two hands taller than her.

She waits and waits, but this figure doesn't move except for the subtle rise and fall of his shoulders. The fog parts some more, and as he starts to leisurely walk toward her, the mist splits around his legs and curls up his back. A sword is held steadily within his grip, and it glistens menacingly.

She backs up a step, nearly tripping over a corpse's leg. Her instincts scream predator, but her head tells her this wouldn't be the best way to attack if he meant her any harm.

"I don't have any coin," she warns him. For a second, she eyeballs the coin on the dirt path. Surely one coin wouldn't cause this much trouble.

The man stops, his chin stooped enough to where she can't even make out his eyes. "I don't want your coin."

Frowning, Nefari blinks. "Then, what do you want." She hates that her voice shakes, but this man, this warrior won't be a sure match like the men lying around her. She knows so, knows by the way he holds himself and the familiar ease in which he grips his sword. Knows so, because his voice is sure and steady.

He's before her now, and he finally lifts his gaze to meet hers. He stares at her from the depths of his cloak. He doesn't answer her but instead says, "I know who you are, Nefari Astra Gala-"

Nefari hisses and then glances around. No one is near, but who in the Divine's name would dare whisper her name out in the open like this? Anyone in this village could be a spy for Urbana and, in turn, a spy for Salix.

But . . .

"Who are you?" she demands. "How do you know who I am?"

"Are you ready to know?"

Ready? By the Divine- "Yes!"

With his free hand, he pushes back his hood. "I would recognize you anywhere, no matter how you shield yourself with your shadows and starlight. I would recognize you as my queen, as our Fate-blessed, as our sword who's meant to cleave the darkness."

Nefari's breath escapes her. "You," she whispers. "You're -" He's exactly as she pictured he'd be with sharp angles, piercing blue eyes, and full lips. "This cannot be real." Emotions crest inside her. Ten years' worth of emotions of grief and sorrow and unearthly relief.

His grin is small but shy and impactful. "It's real. I'm real."

She steps closer to him. "Vale?" A tear slips down her cheek. No. No way this is real. This is a trick of the mind. She's sick. She's demented. She's dreaming. The stress of her life has finally caught up to her.

"Nefari." He cocks his head to the side, and long white hair – as long as hers – spills out from inside his cloak. "Or do you prefer Fari now?"

Her sword clatters to the ground, and she rushes at him. His arms fold around her waist, catching her mid-leap, and she wraps her own arms around his neck. He smells like pine and winter and all things wild, and as she sobs into the crook of his neck, she breathes him in. "You're alive. You're alive!"

He chuckles and grips her tighter. "I am."

"How?" she pulls away from him and peers into his ice-blue eyes. "How are you alive? Where have you been? What happened to you?"

He presses his index finger to her lips, effectively silencing her. "Not here." He grabs her hand. "Come on."

When they're near the water, he tugs her to a stop. The stars shine brightly across the churning bay, but Nefari doesn't marvel at its beauty. Her hand . . . It's holding Vale's. *Vale is alive. He's breathing. He's here.*

Her heart slams against her ribs, and she watches him study the water and the way it laps at the sandy shore. "I never thought I'd see you again," he whispers.

"I didn't even know there was a *you* to see. Ten years, Vale. Ten years!"

"I wasn't sure you were even alive." The words are like a breeze. "Not until recently." He turns and looks around before his eyes find hers again.

Anger hits her then. Anger at feeling abandoned. Anger at grieving her losses when that wasn't entirely the case all along.

"How are you alive, Vale?"

"You're upset." His frown deepens. "Why?"

She throws up her arms. "Because you could have come for me! When you discovered that I was still alive, you could have come for me!"

He shushes her. "Keep your voice down, Fari. There's always – always – someone watching."

"'I know," she spits. She rips her hand from his and tucks both of them under her arms. "You didn't come for me. You - I – I was left alone. I felt alone. I thought you died and I was alone."

"But, I didn't die."

"You said that already," she grinds out.

"This is so confusing." He rubs a spot between his eyebrows.

"Try. Being. Me."

He holds up a finger to silence her. "When I fell off Bastian, I rolled across the floor until I reached your bed. The crones were so busy they didn't realize . . ." He pauses and flicks his gaze over the sand beneath his feet as if his memories are playing across the white grains. "I hid under your bed. Amoon's blood was everywhere, and because of that, they didn't scent me. And when they carried Amoon away –"

"They carried her away?" Nefari is incredulous. She drops her arms to her sides.

He returns his attention to her. "She was alive. Is alive."

"What?" Her voice rises again. He leaps and covers her mouth. She ignores the way his chest pressed to hers sends heat to her cheeks.

"If you do not keep your voice down, I will not be able to tell the story, Nefari," he mutters into her ear. His breath tickles her neck.

Breathing heavily, ready to scream her anger, she nods instead. She can't very well find out the truth if she's beating it out of him.

He doesn't release her mouth, nor does he move away. "She's alive, but she's being kept in Salix as the queen's trophy. She's held in their dungeons, from what my sources tell me."

What Nefari would give to have as many spies as friends as all those seem to have around her. Perhaps she should have asked Patrix to attempt to delve into the Salix matters after all. She's been a fool for not wanting more information about her greatest enemy, but if she can find the crown and discover where the Divine are, perhaps she can get ahead of Queen Seiba Arsonian.

All this pales in comparison to Amoon being alive. To Vale being alive. She shoves the thought away for later evaluation.

Nefari mumbles against his palm.

"If I remove my hand, will you be quiet?"

She nips at his callouses, and he releases her, amusement twinkling in his eyes. "She's alive. . . Amoon is alive. . ."

"Is there an echo?" he asks teasingly. "I swear there's an echo."

He cups his ear, and she slaps his side. "Be serious, Vale." Ten years apart, and they pick up exactly where they left off. It makes her uncomfortable.

He chuckles. "Yes, she's alive, but I do not know in what condition. When she was taken away and sent to Eveland, she was barely breathing." A bone crier swoops overhead, and Vale tugs up the hood of Nefari's cloak and then his own. "Damn things are everywhere."

"Eveland?" she questions, shivering at the sight of the flesh-eating bird.

He frowns. "Salix's crown capital. Do you not recognize the name?"

"I try not to think about Salix too much," she mutters. Shame colors her cheeks. Her mother left a duty to free her people and restore their kingdom, and she's failed to learn basic things about her enemy. Guilt rides her back.

Nefari pushes the hair from her face and paces back and forth in a small line. He watches her and adds, "I'm not alone, Nefari. There are others of the Onyx Guard who survived. They wait and listen in the dead parts of the Frozen Fades forest."

The Onyx Guard was the company of shadow people who guarded the Shadow Kingdom and the royals before it was destroyed. It's shocking to hear the name after a decade, and her guilt dashes as quickly as it came.

"They let you come alone?" she asks, peering at him sidelong while she turns to march the other direction.

"They'll know if something happens to me. The Rebel Legion isn't the only one with a crone on their side."

"Ha!" she chortles half-heartedly. She shouldn't be surprised Vale is as resourceful as Bastian. "How did you survive my mother's blast? How did they survive my mother's blast?"

He slides his hands into the pockets of his cloak. "When they left, I ran from the room. I bumped into Ostin Rutgir, and he and I managed to escape before the blast of magic. Anyone inside the throne room did not survive, but those outside of it . . ."

She taps her arms as she finishes his sentence, "Managed to get to safety."

His jaw flexes solemnly. "We've waited a long time to make our move against the crones - against Salix and their allies. We just didn't know you'd be part of it."

Neither did I, she mumbles inside her head. "Where in the Fade's Forest are they?"

27

The small shake of his head is a punch to her gut. "I cannot tell you."

She stops her pacing to whirl and face him. "Why not?"

"Because it's my job to keep what's left of the new Onyx Guard safe. When my father died . . . They're my responsibility now. My burden."

"They're my people," she challenges. "I'm their queen." The title still tastes foreign on her tongue like she's stealing it from her dead mother.

"Indeed, but their safety comes first. There is a reason no one knows they're alive, and I plan to keep it that way. You've been away a long time, Nefari. Some believe you to still be a rumor, and if I hadn't seen Patrix, I would have never guessed you were alive."

"What do you mean?"

"Didn't he tell you?" He cocks his head to the side. "The pirate queen captured him while he was in the Black Market." He tips his head South East, down the river to where it meets Caws Cove. "She talked about you, though she didn't know your name nor who you . . . really are."

The Pirate Queen? "Luxlynn Billihook? What could she possibly want with Patrix?"

He crosses his arms, and the twinkle in his gaze returns. "Apparently, the two of you stole a horse. *Her*

28

horse. A beloved and cherished horse of white gold and all that nonsense." He said 'beloved and cherished' like some primping courtier gossiping about their love at first sight. "The horse was carrying a saddlebag full of narcotics, ground Diabolus Beetle, I believe. Patrix may be a good spy, but he can't cover his tracks as well as he thinks. Not when he boasts about it while in a drunken stupor at Deeds'. A little coin to Savage Deeds goes a long way in learning things about his patrons."

Rage fills Nefari, and she nearly hisses like a feral rodent. She couldn't care less how he gathered the information. Astra is the Pirate Queen's horse? In truth, she knew that little fact, but Nefari had assumed Astra held no real possession to Luxlynn Billihook. Not to mention she thought the saddlebags were full of money. Patrix led her to believe so, and she graciously handed the saddlebags over to him for his ventures.

Does Patrix realize how potent the drug is? Too much of it, and it kills the user. It's addictive and destructive all at once.

A fool! The satyr is a fool!

"I'm going to kill him." She turns to march back to the inn where everyone is to meet this evening, but Vale's hand on her shoulder stops her.

"No, you won't. He must remain alive."

"Why?" she demands.

29

"Because he is the only one who can walk among the other kingdoms without question. You don't have that luxury." Nefari refrains from telling him that she doesn't need anyone because she knows, deep down, she does. She told Sibyl, over and over again, that she didn't, and in the end, she learned otherwise. He's right. She's right. Nefari can't do this by herself.

"I can at least hurt him."

"There are some relationships you cannot mend after such an act," he whispers. "He is someone you need in the coming days - a tool you cannot refuse." Vale implies her taking her crown, but he doesn't need to know she hasn't decided yet if she'll pick it up or not. Help her people, yes, but be their true queen . . .

Being their queen is different than *calling* herself Queen. She won't stomp on her mother's title in such a way. Not until she can sort it out for herself.

I will not stand in the shadow of my past, she chants to herself.

She recrosses her arms, but the fight leaves her posture as self-doubt curdles the meager contents in her stomach. "I'm still angry with you."

He taps her chin with his finger. "I know, but it was for the best. You'll get over it. And now that things are changing . . ."

She peeks at him from under her lashes, and they say nothing as they stare at one another. He has subtle scars across his face, barely visible upon his pale skin, and briefly, she wonders about the stories of how he got them. Were they deserved? Were they to survive? Or were they a squabble between friends? She asks none of these things.

"You want to meet the others? There are a few more shadow people who survived, and they're traveling with me, for now."

To her shock, he shakes his head. "It's best I remain hidden for a while."

She quirks a brow and cocks out a foot. "You're just going to stalk me, then?"

He smirks. "When did you become so hard and bold?" It was asked teasingly.

"I take pride in my boldness, thank you very much."

"Go on," he murmurs after a moment, tipping his head back to the village. "You should join the others."

"But —"

"No. No buts. Please, Nefari, don't draw attention to the fact that I'm alive. Please, keep this a secret until we both agree it's time."

"I was going to say I wasn't ready to leave you yet," she whispers.

Sighing, he cups a hand at the nape of her neck and brings her forehead to his lips. Against her skin, he says, "I won't be far. I'll never be far."

Warmth spreads to her toes, but when he adds, "I'm yours," it vanishes.

CHAPTER THREE

The warmth from the fire caresses her skin when Nefari enters the inn's tavern. It isn't terribly cold in this village, unlike the mountains, but it's enough to make her nose feel frosty. She gazes about, meets the eyes of a few patrons seated at tables and even the inn's keeper, who pours ale for those seated at the rickety bar.

Beams stretch across the ceiling, and thick posts support them. The floor is dirty with soot from the many fires, and clumps of dirt have been brought in on the boots of patrons coming in from the outdoor elements. The scents of stale ale, horse manure, and body odor reach her nose, and she flares her nostrils to the combined aroma.

Farther beyond the bar is a dark, split hallway. Their small rented rooms are in the back complete with stacked beds to house more than one traveler.

Her gaze swivels to the left. Predictably, Kristal, Kaymen, Cyllian, and Dao are seated at one table in the far corner where the shadows hide their tell-tale shadow people features. Still, their cloak hoods are drawn over their faces.

Their eyes light up when they see her stride to them. With a huff, she sits between Dao and Kristal. "Where are Patrix, Emory, and Fawn?"

Kaymen lifts his clay mug of ale and uses it to point to the hallway. "In their rooms for the night."

"That's too bad. I have it on good authority the spy is a sniveling liar."

"Oh?" Dao curls a brow. "What did he do now?"

"The true question is: What do I have yet to learn?" she murmurs. Dao passes her a full mug, and she lifts it to her parched mouth and greedily gulps. The starch taste coats her tongue, and she grimaces before she sets it back down, half full.

"Fari," Cyllian hisses. "Where did you get that cut?"

She touches her neck. A bead of blood comes away on her fingertips. "I tripped."

Kaymen and Kristal snort, and Kaymen leans into the back of his chair. "Doubtful."

"Truth."

"Lie," Kristal joins in.

"Please, don't fight," Cyllian groans then pins Kristal with a glare. Kristal points at her. "And you don't encourage it. Their bickering down the mountain was enough." She glares at Nefari and Kaymen as good as any chastising. "Honestly, can't you two agree on anything?"

Kaymen and Nefari smirk at each other. Indeed, they had argued the entire way to Calhoun, but their arguments are different than they used to be. Before, they were filled with hatred, envy, and general discontent. Now, it's just a game both participants are willing to play. She finds it fun to openly speak her mind to someone, and she's sure that Kaymen feels the same. Telling Cyllian this would ruin the fun.

They both shrug in response.

Their muffled chatter washes over Nefari as she lets her mind wander. As a child, both she and Amoon had bickered openly, too. Not out of indifference but because they were as close as sisters.

Amoon's alive. Alive! And she can't tell anyone about it.

Nefari touches a dent in the table and traces it with a fingernail. She's always been good at keeping secrets, but this one doesn't feel right. She'll protect Vale though. If she told them about Amoon, she'd have to share where she got the information. They'd catch her lie, and there are already too many lies swimming around, thanks to Patrix.

Sunrise can't come soon enough. She'll confront him, slap him, and demand the truth. The whole truth. How many lies has he told her over the past ten years? He had filled a tiny portion of the hole Amoon once filled, and to find out it's built on a house of lies . . .

"Fari," Dao calls.

"Hmm?"

"Cyllian asked you a question." He frowns and studies her face. "Are you okay? You have murder in your eyes."

She rubs at her eyebrow. "It's been a long journey is all. What was I asked?"

Concern still etched into her expression, Cyllian pitches forward and asks again, "Do you think it's a good idea to split up like Bastian planned? Surely, you need more protection than Kristal in the woods."

"Hey!" Kristal chirps. "That's bloody hurtful."

"Kristal can hold her own," Kaymen defends then belches. Nefari blinks at him. A week ago, he hated her guts.

Kristal must feel the same because she begrudgingly expresses her gratitude. "Thank you, Kaymen."

He drains his ale and then waves to the keeper for a refill. "Don't get a big head about it," he says as the keeper strides in their direction, a pitcher of ale in hand.

"What in the Divine's name is happening here?" Nefari grumbles under her breath, but deep inside, she feels glee. The week's trip down the mountain and to Calhoun, she and Kristal have grown closer together. Nefari even shared parts of her life in the Shadow Kingdom, although she left out anything royal-related.

The keeper, rugged and weather-aged, refills all of their drinks without a word before heading back to the bar and to another waving patron. He had spilled a bit, and Cyllian wipes it away with the sleeve of her cloak. "What do you think, Fari?" she urges softly again.

Twirling her ring on her finger, Nefari blows out a breath. Again, she has the urge to tell them about Vale but bites her tongue. As he implied, he'll follow her to wherever she goes. She hopes she's right on that front because the thought of leaving him behind is not something she'll entertain, and she doubts the group will allow it either. But what is she to tell Cyllian? That she has secret protection?

She wonders what Vale would say if he knew what she was going after and why. Would he still follow? Bringing the others along would make it hard for him to do so. It's a selfish desire, and as a way to protect him, she answers with, "I think we should do as Bastian asked. It won't take much to retrieve my crown. We get in; we get out."

She turns to Kaymen. "The tavern owner agreed to hold Astra and Joana?" Her and Kristal's horses were currently eating their fill of oats and fresh hay.

"He did, but he asked a hefty price for it." Nefari ignores the way his words jabbed. She didn't like leaving her horse behind already.

Bastian didn't just give Nefari coin. He gave them all, minus Kristal, enough to pay for the things they needed on this journey. Kaymen doesn't like spending his own coin on a creature that doesn't belong to him, but with his tone, the option to thank him vanished.

"Then, I'll reserve my thanks to the old coot behind the bar," she snipes.

Silence falls over the group, and when Cyllian yawns and stretches, she stands up. "I'm off to bed. I suggest you all do the same."

Nefari stands with her, pushing her stool backward and her ale forward. "I'll join you."

With the men bunking in one room and the women bunking in another, Nefari wouldn't worry about being woken by anyone walking in. They are grown men. They can go to sleep when they want, and she hopes they wake Patrix in the process. The satyr deserves a restless sleep.

An hour later, sheets and wool pulled to her chin on the top bed above Fawn's, Nefari stares at the crumbling ceiling, thinking of what she will say to him in the morning. Each idea ends with a knife in the thigh, but no matter how much Nefari daydreams of hurting Patrix, as much as she is hurting inside, Vale was right. They need him.

Nefari leans over her bunk and peers down at Fawn's legs half off the bed. Then, she looks to Cyllian on the adjacent bed where her soft snores replace the silence of the night. She slumps back onto the pillow, and eventually, her eyelids drift closed.

And the next morning, when she wakes to the bright, beaming sun through the room's small window, Nefari rises before everyone else and waits outside Patrix's room for him to emerge in search of food.

CHAPTER FOUR

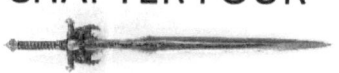

Hair neatly pinned back but clothes rumpled from sleep, Patrix whistles as he shuts his door, nearly jumping from his scruffy skin when he turns to see Nefari standing in the shadows of the inn's hallway. Her arms are crossed, and her eyes are spitting mad.

"You could frighten the hair off a cat, lurking in the shadows like some kind of demon."

And isn't that what she intended?

She marches forward, and with a hand pressed to his chest, she roughly pushes him against the wall.

His expression widens in further surprise. "Nefari?"

"You're a liar. A rotten, foolish, selfish liar."

Patrix peers down the empty hallway. "I don't know what you mean."

"Oh?" she cocks her head mockingly and puts more weight into her hand. He hisses and grips her wrist. "My horse? The saddlebag? The drugs? Ringing any bells, spy of the realm?"

His face softens. "I can explain."

"I really don't think you can," she claims through clenched teeth. "It would just be another lie. Lies, lies, lies. How many more lies, Patrix? How many have you told me?"

He sighs and releases her wrist. "You really ought not to know."

She lets go of him with a chuff. Both Dao and Cyllian emerge from their rooms and pause, taking in the scene before them. She ignores them.

"I cannot trust you. I cannot trust someone who has lied to me my entire life."

"Oh, come on," he beseeches, holding his hands open before him. "I am a spy, Fari. A spy! Did you think I wouldn't lie to you? My job is lying. My life is lying. If it weren't for lies, I'd be dead."

She clenches her fists. "There's still time for that." She moves to slam him back into the wall, but Dao puts a hand between them.

"What's going on?" Dao's voice is deep and gravelly.

"He's a liar." She points at Patrix then glares at Dao. "Did you know? Did you know about the drugs?"

"Drugs?" Cyllian and Dao say together.

"Yes!" She throws her hands up in the air then slams them down on her hips. "Did you know?"

Dao blinks. "No, I had no idea. If I did, I wouldn't have kept it from you."

Rage fuels Nefari's emotions, and the shadows quiver to it in the hall.

"You need to calm down before you alert the other patrons," Patrix whispers, eyeing the flaring shadows with suspicion.

She snarls at him but lowers her volume just the same. "Tell me another of your lies, Patrix. Tell me!"

Patrix's lips form a thin line, and Cyllian says, "Just do it."

He sucks on a tooth and spits out, "The crones know you're alive," like the words are a foul taste in his mouth. "They know the girl they attacked and killed was not you."

The hallway's atmosphere pulls taut. "You told them?"

Patrix thumps the side of his fist against the wall. "I had no choice! I was carrying information they could not have, and when one attacked me in the Shadled, I had no choice!"

"There is always a choice!"

"It wouldn't have mattered, Fari. They already knew!"

She starts pacing, ignoring the innkeeper's wife who lights the torches in the hall. He betrayed her. He's lied to her. And he had no intention of telling her this information before she and Kristal marched into the Shadled Forest riddled with crones seeking shadow people. That was the reason for the Harvest Storm, and there's no way they've stopped their search.

She stops pacing with her back to him. "I won't kill you," she admits begrudgingly, coming to a final decision. "But you and I are done. I do not want to see you again."

And with that, she marches off to the tavern where she knows Kristal is eating her morning meal.

She's done. Absolutely done with the lies.

Dao Pyreswift watches her go before turning back to Patrix with his arms crossed.

"What?" Patrix bites at his inner cheek when Dao says nothing. "What does she want from me?"

"She thought of you as a brother, Patrix. You destroyed that today."

"You betrayed her," Cyllian whispers, hunching her shoulders in defeat. "What did you expect to happen when she learned of it?"

"And what do you think she'll do when she discovers the rest of whatever secrets you still keep? Because we all know when there's one, there's more."

Patrix rubs his hands over his face, scrubbing at his beard. "Kill me, probably."

"Then, maybe you should heed her request and stay away," Dao advises. "Go, wake Emory, and get ready for your journey through Widow's Bay."

Dao steers Cyllian to the tavern, and once they reach it, they stride up to the table Kaymen, Fawn, and Kristal have chosen. Nefari stares at the table angrily while the others watch on with a weary quality.

"Were you going to leave without saying goodbye?" he asks Nefari.

"I can't even talk right now," Nefari murmurs. She hugs herself, and the sight nearly breaks him. At this moment, she seems so small, a quality Nefari has never been since she reached her adult body. She's kept her pain inside for all the years he's known her. To have this effect her so greatly . . .

"She won't tell us what happened," Kristal mutters.

"It's not important," Dao replies, coming to Nefari's defense. He meets the eyes of everyone else when Nefari refuses to meet his own. "What's important right now is that we get ready to move. We can't stay here long. We don't know when the next Salix Army will make an appearance."

"And the horses?" Kristal questions.

"Paid for, remember?" Kaymen supplies. "You and Nefari's horses will stay here while you journey, and we will take our own to the Black Market."

"I still don't understand why they can't go into the Shadled," she grumbles.

"You cannot bring them." Kaymen touches her hand. "You've never been in the Shadled. They'll attract too much attention from the beasts within."

"If you paid off our horses to stay for so long, how did you afford our own stay last night?" she asks him, frowning.

Dao tries to hide his grin. "He sold Patrix's and Emory's horses to the inn's keeper. It'll be enough for several weeks' worth of boarding, and his wife was happy with the transaction."

"You sold them?" Cyllian asks, incredulous.

"It's not like they're going to need them," Kaymen says defensively. He removes his hand from Kristal's, lifts his fork, and digs into his eggs. "They're headed on a ship to Loess. There's one going to be docked at Caw's Cove, full of fish. It's to return two moons from today to deliver the bounty to Vivian, Urbana's Capital."

Fawn points her fork at the entire group. "Just enough time to get there, then."

"Indeed."

"Why not take a boat down instead?" Kristal asks. "Surely, someone here has a boat you can take down to Widow's Bay."

"Pirates," they all mumble, and Dao adds, "Occasionally, they travel this far north of the river to plunder the nearby villages. If they were to catch one of us, we'd be sold."

Heat rises to Kristal's cheeks. "Oh. Well, what about this village? How does it still stand?"

Nefari is the one who answers, "Because they pay them off, which is why this place takes a great deal of coin just for a night's rest."

Placing her fork back on the table after one last bite, Fawn stretches her arms over her head, drains her drink, and prepares to move away from the table. "I'll check the weapons over and make sure they're cleaned and sharpened. The salty air of Widow's Bay will destroy them."

"I'll grab our saddlebags." Cyllian, who still stands next to Dao, breaks away from the group and follows Fawn to the hallway, weaving and skirting around customers waiting for their meal. Some stare at Fawn, having not seen a Kadoka centaur before, but at least, they don't cause any trouble.

"I'll gather the horses," Kaymen quips, sliding off his chair. "We better hope the favor Savage owes Bastian is a good one. I don't like making deals with the old King of the Pirates."

"Bastian wouldn't have said so if it wasn't," Nefari murmurs. She raises her gaze to meet his, but her voice sounds so small.

Dao reaches to rub her arm. "We'll see each other soon, then," he whispers to her when Kaymen is gone.

She nods, and he turns her to pull her into a hug. "Shine bright, but only when you need to," he murmurs, kissing the top of her head. "Only when you must."

"I will," she promises.

He releases her as Emory approaches, his appearance ruffled. His eyes have dark circles underneath them, and the cloth wrapped around his head is tilted. Dark brown hair peeks out from underneath.

While trying to unsuccessfully hide his grin, Dao raises an eyebrow at him. "Didn't sleep well?"

"Patrix snores." He rubs at his eyes then peers at the table blearily. "I hear they have excellent eggs. I saw the large coop out back and heard them holler at the sun this morning. Is that true? The eggs, I mean."

"I wouldn't know," Dao supplies.

"Before you go and order some of them," Nefari says to Emory, "You're sure Urbana cannot be switched to the Legion's side?"

On the way down the mountain, he had said as much. Salix has Urbana in more ways than the Urbanian King's infatuation with the Salix Queen.

"They will never leave the slave trade, Fari," he whispers to her.

She nods and touches his arm. "I just wanted to make sure. Please, have a safe journey. And throw Patrix overboard when you have a chance."

He chuckles. "I will. Though, you do know that satyrs cannot swim, yes?"

Her grin is feral, though her eyes are still sad. "I'm counting on it." And with that, Nefari heads to their room to gather their belongings, Kristal right behind her.

"I told him his secrets would be his end, but he didn't listen to me," Emory says to Dao while the two of them watch the woman disappear into the hall. "Is she going to be okay?"

"She has to be," he murmurs. A sinking feeling fills his gut. Sighing, he turns back to Emory. The inn keeper's wife sets two plates of eggs in front of Dao and Emory, grabs the empty plates, and scuttles off to fulfill another order.

"Did you order this?" Dao asks him.

Emory shrugs and picks up his fork. "I was hungry, and you didn't have a plate, and . . . Well, I was trying to be nice."

"Eat quickly. Kaymen is already gathering the horses."

He shovels eggs into his mouth, and around a mouthful of food, he mutters, "Look, I mean it about Urbana. If Nefari wants to take back her kingdom, it won't be with their help. Maybe Patrix can talk his father into it, but -"

"His father?"

"Yes. He's ah- He's the Loess's Queen's brother. He has the ear of his sister."

"My sweet Divine," Dao curses. "Does Bastian know?"

"I'd guess so."

Indeed, Patrix has kept much from everyone. Dao rubs at his neck. "Look, while you're there, do you think you can - "

"Talk to Loess and see if they're supporting the Legion?"

"Do you think they would?"

"I had already planned to ask, right after I beg the mother for her daughter's hand."

Dao releases a breath. "That's a tall order."

He shrugs. "She's bound to agree to one of them."

CHAPTER FIVE

With the sun fully risen, Kristal jogs to keep up with Nefari as they move away from Calhoun and march across the fields of crops that stretch from there to the Shadled. The crops are brittle twigs poking from the frozen ground, having been harvested before the snow fell at the beginning of winter. Nefari doesn't avoid them as she marches along.

"Will you slow down?" Kristal asks, her accent thick.

"I want as far away from here as I can get."

"Fari, what happened?" She tugs Nefari to a stop.

Nefari obeys with a huff, peeks at Kristal, and grinds her teeth as she stares into her friend's brown eyes. They're soft, cautious, and sympathetic. Nefari wonders how her own look if her inner turmoil and sense of betrayal is anything to go by.

But she knows, deep down she *knows* Kristal would never cut so deep, would never betray her in such a way that their friendship would shatter into a million pieces.

"Everywhere I turn, I'm betrayed," she finally answers.

Kristal turns her head away. Her red cheeks shine in the sun, and Nefari doesn't know if it's the rays or a blush. "What do you mean?"

"The crones are searching for me, and he told them I'm alive." Kristal's blush disappears as rage transforms her expression.

"Do you want me to kill him? I'll kill him." She moves to turn back toward the village, but Nefari knows she'd never catch up to them. The group had left on their horses the moment Nefari and Kristal had begun their journey.

A grin spreads across Nefari's face. "You would, wouldn't you."

She smirks. "In a heartbeat."

Nefari moves to keep walking but, this time, much slower. "No death will be had today. We have a duty to complete."

Kristal strides by her side. "Why do they want you?"

Nefari looks at her sidelong. "Because they want the Queen's crown, and they think I can get it."

"You truly think this crown will show you where the other Divine are? Fate-blessed, Hope-favored, and Choice-chosen?

It's Nefari's turn to blush. Blush because, by not telling Kristal, her good friend, exactly who she is and that she's Fate-Blessed, she's lying by omission. There will be a time when she has to tell Kristal, but that day is not today. Though she's growing closer to the girl with each passing day, she won't divulge that information. Not yet. Not when much hangs in the balance.

It makes her feel sick to her stomach, both for knowing she's lying and for having to admit who she truly is to the only person who has wanted nothing from her except a kinship. It makes her no better than Patrix, but at least, her lie won't hurt anyone emotionally. At least, not yet.

"No," she finally grumbles because it is the only truth she can tell. "But it doesn't hurt to try." *Even if it'll hurt to go into the kingdom itself*.

Seeming to think the same, Kristal asks, "Are you ready to go home?"

She pauses, licks her lips, and decides to answer with another truth. "No." Because she's not.

"You'll forgive him, you know."

"Patrix? Over my dead body."

"Can you really just end a friendship so easily?"

"He lied to me. Lied about the crones being after me. The Divine only knows what they want from me, aside from the crown."

"They'll see you dead, once you have the crown."

"Crones tend to do that," Nefari grumbles.

There's a pause, a silence aside from their feet crunching against the dead crops, until Kristal exclaims, "You will. You'll forgive him."

Two days after leaving Nefari and Calhoun behind, Dao and his group finally reach the edge of the Black Market and weed their way through the crowd. The Black Market is more teaming than Dao would have ever expected. People travel in droves from one tent or table to the next, and the sound of their voices is loud to his ears. He's never been to the Black Market, but this is beyond what he had expected.

"I'll tie the horses at Deeds'," Kaymen says as they all dismount. He grabs the reins of each horse while Emory stretches his legs, having awkwardly dismounted Fawn's back. Patrix had been subjected to walking the entire way, and for that, Dao believes he deserves the hardship and disadvantage.

Their ride here had been quiet and uneventful, empty without Nefari and Kristal and Kaymen's usual banter. Dao found himself missing the quipped taunts and verbal jabs, but at least it's slightly warmer in the Black Market than Calhoun had been. The salty air is thick, just like Fawn had predicted, and the humidity is enough to feel slapped in the face by a chilly wet cloth. It makes his tunic and trousers stick to his body in all of the uncomfortable places.

Dao turns to Patrix, who awkwardly shifts his weight behind them. Exhaustion shows in the way he holds himself. "Are you coming into Deeds'?"

Patrix shakes his head. "I'm not going near that lunatic."

"More secrets?" Dao glares at him.

"Something like that," Emory murmurs as he straightens the cloth on his head.

"Now, don't be like this," Patrix grumbles. "My secrets are mine to tell."

"Your secrets are what will get you killed," Fawn barks. "You're going to take others down with you, and then what, Patrix? How will your secrets fair then?" When she learned of what had transpired between him and Fari, she had been ready to dump Emory and tackle Patrix to the ground. Strangely, Kaymen's urging at peace was the only thing that kept him on his own two legs.

Patrix wiggles his jaw as he considers Fawn's anger. There's nothing he can say to bank the woman's rage; this Dao knows.

"Come on," Emory urges gently, tugging on Patrix's dirty sleeve. "They'll be boarding the ship soon. If we don't go now, we'll have to wait another week for another shipment to come in."

Reluctantly, Patrix nods, but before he leaves, he says, "I may have many secrets, but trust me when I say this: Do not trust Savage. I don't care what favor he owes Bastian. He will not hesitate to turn you over to the Divine knows what if it so suits him."

"Thank you, Patrix," Cyllian whispers. He nods again, and Emory steers him away.

"Do we trust his word?" Fawn questions when the crowd swallows them both.

"Yes." Dao answers. "He may be a liar, but he wouldn't caution unless it was prudent. Come on. Let's get this over with."

The group makes their way through the crowd, hoods pulled over their heads, as they head toward Deeds'.

When they're in front of the door, and Kaymen is tying the last horse, Dao mutters, "Cyllian and I will go inside. The rest of you wait by the horses. I don't trust this crowd to not take off with them as soon as there's nobody watching."

Fawn and Kaymen move to guard the horses without argument, and Cyllian breathes, "Ready?"

Dao doesn't answer. He grabs Cyllian's warm hand and dips inside.

Before their eyes can adjust to Deeds' dark and quiet interior, they're grabbed. Cyllian squeaks, and Dao yells as his upper arms are roughly grasped. The back of his knees are kicked, and they slam onto the unforgiving planks.

When his eyes adjust, he witnesses one particular man pointing the tip of his knife at Cyllian's throat.

"Don't touch her!" Dao threatens, tugging against his captor's hold.

The sound of wood thumping against the floor greets them, and a figure emerges from behind the bar's deep shadows. The man is older, scarred across his face, and his wooden leg stands out when he makes his way to their side.

"Savage Deeds," Dao spits. Rage boils his blood. "By the divine, what are you doing? Let her go!" He didn't care so much about himself as he did Cyllian. Sweet Cyllian doesn't deserve to be threatened by anyone.

"Did you think I wouldn't recognize a shadow person when I saw one?" As soon as he finishes the sentence, their hoods are removed, leaving their white hair gleaming despite the lack of light.

Dao struggles once more, trying to rip his arms away from the men so he can choke the life out of Savage. He'd do it. For Cyllian - for one of his own - he'd do it.

One large man grabs him by the collar, pulls him to his feet, and shoves him against the wall. Dao slams his forehead against the man, and the man stumbles back, releasing Dao. The other two rush him, and Dao dodges and weaves.

The dagger-wielding man holding Cyllian shouts, "Oy! Do you want me to slit her throat? I'll do it! I'll do it in a heartbeat!"

It was enough of a distraction for Dao to pause, and then a fist connected to his jaw. The two men capture him once more, and Dao is shoved back onto his knees, hair gripped and forced to gaze at Savage Deeds.

Savage has his arms crossed, his dark skin gleaming from the dim torchlight hooked to a pillar to his left. His clothes are neat as if freshly bought but dull in color like the inside of his tavern.

His scars dance when he smirks. "What makes you think I won't march you onto my daughter's pretty boat and have you shipped off to Salix as slaves?"

Dao spits blood onto the floor, eyeing Savage's wooden leg. He raises his spiteful gaze. "Your daughter hates you."

"Enough to not take what I offer?" Savage's thick brow quirks. "She and I are seeing eye-to-eye on certain matters these days, one of them to bring her the captives she so desires, or did your satyr spy not tell you so?"

Dao can't help but wonder what bargain was struck between the two because the legends say she hates his guts. She had thrown him overboard the Wench, the most feared pirate ship of Widow's Bay, when she named herself Pirate Queen. What sort of man would go back to a daughter like that?

As for Patrix, well, he'd see him regret not divulging that tidbit of information before he departed from the group.

There's a rustle to Dao's left. Both Savage and he look as Cyllian elbows the man in the gut, ducks from the knife's sharp edge, and spins out of her captor's grasp. Her punch to his face sends a cracking sound through the tavern, but she grabs the man's dagger before he falls onto his rump.

Dao blinks as she straightens herself and her cloak and turns to Savage. Through clenched teeth, she bites out, "Do not think, for one moment, Bastian Pike hasn't had a hand in each of our training." She points the dagger at him, showing a side of her Dao has never seen. Her voice is steady as she adds, "And do not think we came alone."

A deep laugh comes from the depths of Deeds'. "Little puppet, I would wager that was your first real brawl."

She jabs the dagger in his direction and emphasizes each word, "I know about what you did to Bastian." She steps closer, slightly threatening. "The healers talk, Mr. Deeds. Do you want me to tell your friends about the love you destroyed between the Leader of the Rebel Legion and your daughter? Or perhaps what Patrix knows? The part about who your daughter really is?"

Savage squints his eyes at her, chewing over what she said. What she promised.

Secrets? Dao could be rich if he had a coin for every secret told since they left Kadoka City, but it stings a little that she hadn't shared any with him. He feels in the dark, a sensation that makes him clench his fists by his knees.

He didn't know Bastian was in love with the Pirate Queen, nor does he know who the Pirate Queen really is.

"You will say nothing on either front if you know what's good for ya."

She squares her jaw, and it makes her seem much taller. "Then, release my friend, or I'll explain, in depth, who her mother is. Satyrs like to gossip, Mr. Deeds. Though gentle in nature, Patrix is cunning and told me everything on the way here."

Dao blinks again. He had wondered why they hung back from the group during their journey from Calhoun. He had noticed the small talk, but never had he thought Patrix was spilling such a vital secret. He planned to ask Cyllian what she held over Savage's head as soon as she was able. Demand it. He'd demand the answers.

The men around them shift their weight uncomfortably. Savage says nothing.

"Release. My. Friend."

Savage snarls. "Your threats will get you a one-way ticket to the slave ships someday, little girl." Despite his words, he nods to his men, and roughly, they toss Dao to the ground.

"That'll be all, boys," he says to them.

Dao climbs to his feet, and Cyllian passes him the dagger then crosses her arms as the men slowly return to their tables, grumbling all the way.

A bit leery, Savage asks, "What is it you want?"

"We're here to collect a favor from Bastian Pike," Dao growls. He scoots closer to Cyllian and has half a mind to wrap her in his arms and carry her away from Savage Deeds. She has no idea the target she painted on her back. Savage Deeds is not a man who will take threats lightly.

Dao continues, "We need you, a ship, and a crew to take us to Hope's Island."

"When?"

Dao raises both eyebrows. "Now. I want to be away from the Black Market by sundown."

Savage cracks his knuckles. "And who do you propose man's the ship."

"Everyone owes you favors, Savage. I'm aware of how you work. You'll think of something."

He grins. "You're not going to like the company I keep."

"It's better than no company at all."

CHAPTER SIX

Night falls outside the Shadled Forest, which means nothing to the inside of the forest. It's as dark in the day as it is after dusk, and tonight is no exception. The only thing lighting the space around Kristal and Nefari is a pathetic little fire. Kristal had complained about it, but big fires attract attention, and though they'd provide a much-appreciated warmth, they couldn't chance it.

Trees upon trees hug the outer edges of their tentless camp. The trunks are close together in this part of the forest, a fact Nefari is finding cumbersome. They spend more time crawling over protruding roots than actually walking, but tonight, they found space to sleep.

Diabolus Beetles cling to their trunks, glowing dully. Kristal had watched them for a while and desired to touch one until Nefari put the fear of the Divine into her. As soon as Nefari told her she would die, Kristal immediately lost interest.

Beyond their circle of trees is … well, Nefari can't see beyond the trunks. Not with the fire's small glare and beetles' glow. It's a fact she's grateful for. The Shadled can feel haunting to anyone who isn't used to it. Truth be told, she's been away from it so long that she isn't used to it either. She isn't sure how she feels about it, about the haunting forest that no longer feels familiar or the soundless night that raises the hair on her arms.

She looks back to her inferaze sword, the tip propped against a stone embedded in the dry soil. She pulls out a rag from her cloak's inner pocket, props a foot next to the blade's tip, and begins to clean the blade itself. It's not dirty, but she finds the action soothing when her nerves are on edge.

Asleep, Kristal lies on the cracked and dry dirt next to the fire. Her soft breathing is a hum in the background, but Nefari keeps one ear on the forest. A lot of good it will do them, though; all she hears is the crackling of the small fire, but that doesn't mean she - they - are not being watched. Creatures lurk here, and not just the elusive crones.

They've been traveling for a few days if their stench is anything to go by, and not once have they met a single crone, wraith, or bone crier. It's a miracle in itself but also a suspicious one. Nefari doesn't like the way it curls a sense of wrongness inside her. It's like the Shadled is holding its breath, waiting for what might happen next.

When soft snores come from Kristal, Nefari stuffs the rag back inside her cloak and turns to her left. Removing the shadows from her hair and her face, she whispers into shadows around her, a message to Sibyl about where they're at and a rough estimate of how many days they have left in their journey.

There's no point in hiding who she is here. There's no point in denying who she is and stows away her true features with a sliver of magic. Not if she wants to go home and see what's left of it. It would be a disservice to pretend she isn't the princess - the fated queen of her prophecy, but it still stings to think about it. She still feels like she is stealing what her mother was to the realm: a beacon of hope.

But, without the shadows, she feels naked. Exposed. In danger. She works to squash the feelings down, ignores the urge to replace the shadows, and finishes her message to Sibyl instead.

When she's done, she exhales softly. It does nothing for her anxiety.

They have another few days' walk before they reach the shadows that'll take them to the kingdom's edge. She could shadow jump there. She could take Kristal, leap through the shadows, and reach it in the next hour, but she hasn't shadow jumped since that day in the forest with her mother, just before her eighth birthday. She isn't about to try it on her friend.

The closer they get to those shadows, the more Nefari wants to turn back. Questions have replayed over and over again since the barren crop fields. Where are all the promised crones? What will she do when they get there? What will she see? Will she fall to her knees in the ash, or will she hold her head high and endure the reign of silence and the sprinkle of bone dust?

From her seat, Nefari studies Kristal and the way she sleeps. Her hands are tucked under her face, and despite the dark, she can clearly see the purple bruises of exhaustion under her eyes.

Throughout the journey, Kristal has had her own questions about the kingdom, most of which Nefari cannot remember nor does she want to discuss. If she is being honest with herself, she *can't* discuss them.

She hasn't told Kristal she walks beside the Queen of the Shadow People, either. She hasn't told her she is the fated princess whom everyone believes dead. Everyone . . . except for the crones, apparently.

With a pinch of her ring between her fingers, she shoves the risen thought of Patrix's betrayal aside. She had told herself she'd let it go, but she has yet to actually do so. After all, she's lying to Kristal by omitting the truth too, and now she's stuck with the idea of how she's going to break the news without hurting her friend. There was no easy way for Patrix to divulge what he'd done, and there's no easy way for Nefari to, either.

The Diabolus Beetles take flight and disappear into the forest a second before a low whistle comes from behind her. She nearly jumps out of her skin. She recognizes the whistle's tune, however. It was one Vale used to make when they snuck through the Shadow Kingdom's castle.

Slowly, soundlessly, she stands and slides her inferaze blade into its sheath. She climbs over the nearest root and tentatively strides into the darkness.

Away from the fire, her vision adjusts. She can see well in the dark just as all shadow people can, but not *that* well. Not like the Shadled's predators.

She cautiously prowls anyway. She only has to travel a few trees down before she sees Vale's silhouette leaning against a trunk, arms crossed over his chest.

"I didn't think you were following us," she whispers, keeping her voice low enough to not wake Kristal. "But I shouldn't be surprised you're as stealthy as a mountain cat."

"That's a habit born from living in the Fades."

When she stands before him, she studies his scowl. "What's wrong?"

"Why are you traveling in the Shadled? Why are you going home?"

She crosses her arms, cocks a foot out, and matches his defensive posture. "It's a queen's duty to return home."

"Fari," he growls softly, truly a predator in his own right. "What you're doing is dangerous. No shadow person has returned since the day it was invaded. Tell me why. And tell me who the human is. She seems . . . off. Weak."

Nefari decides to answer his last question with a glance back to the soft fire and its reflection dancing across the trunks. "Her name is Kristal, and she's not weak." The memory of her saving Nefari's life comes to mind and the fact she hasn't made one complaint for the entire journey. "She's afflicted by an incurable illness. The journey has been hard on her."

"Weak it is, then."

She turns her attention back to Vale. "She's here to help me. And as for your first question, not that it's any of your business -"

"Anything about the shadow people is my business."

"You're not their queen," she challenges.

"Neither are you. Not until you see your people freed."

She hisses at him, a sound that would make any stray feline proud. "What do you want me to do? March to Salix and cut their chains with my sword?" They both know she can't do that. It's more complicated than that.

His jaw ticks. "Tell me what you're doing now."

She searches his face and softens her own. He's right; he does have the right to know. With their adolescent promise to marry one another, he would have been king by now and deserving of the truth, but in this moment, this thought does not comfort her. There's a good chance he'll fight her over the matter. Vale wouldn't be Vale if he didn't.

"I'm retrieving my mother's crown."

He loosens an arm to point at her. "Your crown."

"So, *now* I'm queen?" She quirks a brow.

"I didn't say so, but by blood right, it is yours." He tips his head to the side. "Why are you retrieving it?"

She blows out a pent-up breath and leans against the tree with him. "Because the pirates, the crones, and Salix are working together to find it."

He closes his eyes and chuckles. The revolution is clear in his expression. "So, that's what's going on. We couldn't find the connection, nor why they banded together so tightly." He opens his eyes and adds fiercely, "There was an army marching to the Fades, and we had no idea why."

"Well, now you know," she grumbles. "Kristal was part of the army's servants."

"She's from Salix?" he grinds out. "How could you -"

69

Nefari holds up a hand. "Don't. She saved my life."

It's his turn to search her face. "Tell me what really happened to you - what made you so hard."

She runs a hand through her hair and tucks it behind an ear. "That's a conversation that will take time to tell."

He settles in against the tree. "I have time."

Of course he does. She grins a small grin and dives into everything that's happened to her since the day their kingdom fell. She tells him about Sibyl, about Fawn, about Bastian, Dao, Kaymen, and all the others. She tells him about her lessons with Bastian and their missions to save villages. He listens intently even when she tells him about the deaths, nearly choking out the words. Even when she recounts the Harvest Storm and everything they lost in those few long minutes it happened.

When she's finished, he brings up a hand and cups the side of her face. He doesn't need to say anything. The way he rubs his thumb over her cheekbone says it all.

At that moment, she's reminded about how much she's missed him, reminded of how much they've missed together. He was supposed to be hers forever, and her heart still longs for him even if he's a stubborn male and they're both different people than they first set out to be.

She wants to tell him this, but . . .

She opens her mouth to do so anyway.

Vale barely moves out of the way when a dagger embeds in the trunk between their heads. His hand flies to the pommel of his sword, and he peers into the inky darkness. Nefari needn't guess who threw it, because she recognizes the hilt.

Kristal stomps their way, another dagger poised. Her glaring line of sight is set on Vale.

Nefari jumps between her and Vale and holds her hands up placatingly. "He's a friend, Kristal! A friend!"

She stops in her tracks. "A friend?" she nearly shrieks. "He was choking you!

"What?" Nefari nearly laughs but looks back to where Vale and herself had been huddled, his hand on her . . . "He wasn't choking me."

"Yeah? If he's such a friend, how come I've never seen him before?" She weighs the dagger with her fingertips. "And - And all the shadow people are enslaved!"

Nefari shakes her head. "Not all." She moves aside so Kristal can get a second glance at her target. "This is Vale Riversdale. He was - um -" she scratches her cheek.

"I was her intended," Vale finishes with an edge of annoyance in his tone. "And while you're awake and having learned of my existence, do you mind telling me what you were doing with the army who headed to the north?"

"Vale!" Nefari barks. "She was as much a slave as our own people. She was the princess's servant from birth until her escape!"

Vale flinches as if struck. "The army had the princess?"

"Yes," both women say, though Kristal's answer is a bit more meek compared to her own.

He steps away from the tree and grips his sword tighter. "We should have intercepted when we had the chance. One less Salix royal would have been better for the entire realm." Kristal looks away, shame rising in her expression. Vale doesn't miss it. "What do you know? Why are Luxlynn Billihook and the crones partnering with Salix?"

"I don't know much," she whispers.

Vale marches past Nefari, grabs Kristal by the collar of her cloak, and pushes her back against a tree trunk, suspending her a foot or two off the ground. The tip of Kristal's dagger touches the underside of Vale's jaw, but he pays no attention to it.

"Vale!" Nefari cautions again. "She's innocent."

He ignores her. "Tell me what you know."

Kristal glares at him from down her nose. "Only that the Pirate Queen would visit a few times a year."

Nefari halts from going to rescue her. *She'd visit?* Nefari hadn't heard the rumor, and briefly, she wonders if Patrix knows and had decided not to tell her - tell the Legion.

"Why? Tell me the truth or I'll -"

"Because she's my sister."

He slowly releases her. "Your sister? Luxlynn is of Salix blood?"

She straightens her cloak. "We share the same mother."

Nefari exhales a slow breath. "Kristal's father is the Red Reaper."

Kristal peers past Vale's head and turns her glare on Nefari. "Thanks. Thanks so much."

She shrugs. "I won't keep secrets from him."

"Who is Luxlynn's father if it is not your own?" Vale presses.

"There are rumors in the castle that she is the daughter of Savage Deeds."

Vale shakes his head. "The old bastard. The lying old bastard. How are you still alive? How did the famed Rebel Legion keep from killing you?"

"Because they don't know everything," Nefari murmurs truthfully.

Vale whips around to face her. "You kept the truth from Bastian? For Salix blood?"

"Some of it." Nefari holds her head high. "Besides, blood means nothing."

He snarls and shakes his head. "Then you're a fool."

Wetting her lips, she smirks. "That I am."

He runs a hand through his white and long hair, closing his eyes for a moment before turning back to Kristal. "Who does Luxlynn visit with when she comes to Salix?"

Kristal frowns. "The queen, of course."

"Wasn't that obvious?" Nefari asks. "She's not lying to you, Vale. She saved my life. Why would she save my life only to continue to lie?"

"People lie all the time," he grinds out. "You lie by omission. I lied by keeping my livelihood a secret. Bastian lied to your mother to keep you alive. Everyone lies. She is no exception."

"Leave it!" she barks at him. "She's here to stay and here to help me."

"Then you're both fools for thinking one isn't lying to the other."

Nefari stiffens, praying he doesn't spill her secret. It's clear he knows she hasn't told Kristal, and though they're swapping truths, this isn't one she's ready to share.

Kristal looks at Nefari. "I assume he'll be traveling with us from now on?"

She nods, and Vale proclaims, "You bet on the Divine's name I will be."

"Lovely." Kristal moves past Vale and retrieves her dagger from the tree's trunk, sliding both back against her hip. "Then, I'll prepare myself for a terrible journey with terrible company," she adds while heading back to the fire. Vale follows her, leaving Nefari in the dark, mind whirling and heart pounding.

That was close. Too close.

CHAPTER SEVEN

The next morning, Vale's sword clashes against Nefari's inferaze blade. She hops back, shoulders bumping against the trunk of a tree barely visible if it wasn't for a sliver of the campfire's light.

"That was a cheap shot!" she barks, propelling herself forward.

From where she watches just outside their fighting ring, Kristal laughs softly to herself. She's been watching them contentedly, refusing to get in on the action for a "better view at where this turn will take the both of them."

He parries her strike with one of his own then shoves her back once more. They've been sparring from the moment they woke, Vale having demanded it. She wonders if he had done so to see if she was capable of caring for herself, and as she spars with him, she's beginning to wonder herself. Every move she makes, he's one step ahead.

"It's not a cheap shot if I were your enemy, Fari." He slams his blade into hers, and sparks fly. Swords crossed, he leans his weight into her. The sweat beaded at her temple trickles over her cheek as he says, "You're wild. Undisciplined. It's a miracle Bastian taught you anything."

"I am not wild."

"Oh, yes you are," Kristal chirps. "You should have seen her in the city, Vale. She-"

"Bite your tongue!" Nefari shouts at her. Kristal hides her grin by tucking her bottom lip between her teeth.

"As wild as the beasts in this forest." He hooks a leg around hers, and they topple to the ground. Vale straddles her before she can roll out of the way. She tries to wiggle out from underneath him, but his thighs hold her tight.

"If I could use my magic, you'd be bacon," she growls.

He nips her chin and mumbles, "You like bacon if I remember correctly."

Kristal rolls her eyes and pushes off the tree she was leaning against. "Before you two make puppy eyes at each other, I'll excuse myself and go pack our belongings."

Nefari turns back to Vale and glares up at him. "I am not undisciplined. Bastian -"

"Oh, don't you start with the Bastian excuse. I know you, remember? You're a rule-breaker, and that hasn't changed over time."

Anger curdles Nefari's blood, and the shadows the fire makes leap and bend. He looks at them with wonder in his eyes. "Is that you? Can you move the shadows?"

"I'm not telling," she says petulantly.

He returns his attention with a smirk then taps the tip of her nose. "Wild."

"And don't you adore it." The words were child-like, immature, and mocking all wrapped into one, but Nefari doesn't care. He bested her. *Bested* her. Nobody bests her.

He pulls the short dagger from her hip, and she hisses when he presses it to her throat above the scab formed there. "Untamed. Tell me, Nefari, are you just this way around me or around everyone?"

She says nothing and snaps her jaw shut instead.

His scent tugs at her anger when he leans closer, nose to nose. "Are you distracted because I'm here?"

"No," she whispers, knowing it to be a partial lie. In truth, everything is distracting her.

"Mmhmm," he hums.

"Don't flatter yourself. You would be distracted too if you were me," she says instead of having to explain all of her feelings. She's already not fond of the feelings, so why burden him with them. It'll only make him worry. She doesn't want him to worry.

The shadows return to their slumber as her anger leaves her body. She slumps against the dry dirt, mutely admitting defeat.

"Being distracted will get you killed." A serious expression takes over the flirtatious edge to his firm lips. "Now, tell me. Can you truly move the shadows?"

She licks her bottom lip and blows out a breath. "Maybe. I don't know. I've never tried. They move whenever I'm upset."

"How long has this been happening?"

"Forever." She huffs a half-hearted laugh.

"You never told me about them when we were children."

"Yeah, well." She blows hair out of her face. "I never told my parents, either."

"And does Kristal know?"

She shakes her head, hair tugging against something in the dirt.

"Good." The word is sultry, and it curls Nefari's toes. "What else can you do?"

"Everything my mother could. I have a sword, too. Not this one." She holds up the sword in her hand. "It's made of hot starlight. I killed a wraith with it."

He nods slowly, remembering what she told him last night. "What else?"

"That's all I know."

"That's it?"

"Well, I haven't exactly had the means to practice," she mocks. "Wraiths and bone criers, remember?"

"Can the wraiths detect your shadows?"

"No. They've never come when the shadows move."

He licks his lips thoughtfully. "Your grandmother was said to be able to move her shadow like a second person. Perhaps this is an extension of that."

"It's different," she corrects, slumping her hand back to the ground, sword clinking against a root. "The shadows are . . . living, almost. And I don't know what they want from me."

"What does your crone say?" he asks, leaning in close until his lips nearly touch hers.

Breathlessly, she divulges, "She believes it to be an extension of my Divine magic."

"I believe her right." His lips feather against hers, and her toes curl in their boots. What he does to her, Nefari has never felt. "Don't fear the gift, Nefari."

And just like that, the moment ends. He releases her and stands, hand outstretched to pull her up. She takes it, rises, and dusts off her trousers with her free hand. "In the Shadow Kingdom, I want you to see if you can use them to help you."

She opens her mouth to retort, but quicker than the eye can see, he hurls her dagger. It passes over her shoulder and flips about behind her. She hears the thud, then a squeal, and whirls to peer into the darkness. A short, four-legged beast, one of thick fur, jagged teeth, and massive snout, falls to a heap on the ground, her knife embedded in its eye.

"What the bloody Divine was that?" she hears Kristal shout.

"A Yorkmire." Whirling back to Vale, Nefari frowns. "How did you see that?"

"I lived in the Fades, remember? I heard it." He laughs when her frown deepens, a great belly laugh. The tension between them snaps when he adds, "Breakfast, anyone?"

Nefari's stomach grumbles its agreement.

Having eaten and put out their fire, Vale, Nefari, and Kristal set off into the darkness. Nefari doesn't want to spend any more nights in the Shadled than she has to. This forest is tainted with memories, and just because they've only encountered one beast, that doesn't mean there aren't more.

It isn't long before Kristal begins to struggle with their packs, tripping over boulders and slowly making her way over roots.

"Are you going to be okay?" Nefari takes the packs for herself and trades Kristal the inferaze sword.

"I will, but how much longer?" Nefari gives a sympathetic smile to Kristal's question.

"You trust her enough to carry your blade?" Vale hisses.

"Yes!" she barks at him. She shoulders the packs then marches past him to take the lead. Kristal nearly shoves her shoulder into him as she catches up with Nefari. Nefari peers at her, then peers again; because, in her hand, the blade seems to . . . glow.

"How are you doing that?" Nefari questions her softly.

"Pardon?" Kristal follows her gaze. "Oh. I don't know."

"It's made of inferaze," Vale explains behind them. "Divine magic."

Nefari peers over her shoulder. "How do you know about inferaze?"

"Do you honestly think you're the only one who does? I was in the market, searching for the dealer at one point."

Nefari turns and walks backward. "Did you ever find him?" Vale shakes his head, and Nefari turns back around, climbing over a root after Kristal. "Do you feel the magic?" she asks her.

"A little," Kristal reluctantly admits. "It feels . . . alive. Like it's breathing life into me."

"And your illness?"

Kristal's longing gaze does not go unnoticed, and Nefari remembers what Sibyl had cautioned her about like an echo in her mind.

Sibyl had thought Kristal was drawn to the sword and might use it to bargain with her life if she were ever sent back to Salix as a traitor. And now, Nefari wonders if she'd done the right thing by giving it to her.

Perhaps Sibyl had assumed wrong. Perhaps Kristal only wants it to feel normal. After all, the night she saved Nefari, and right after she killed the harvestman, Nefari had seen the same wondrous expression as she does now.

They duck under a low branch as Kristal says, "All but gone," in a wispy, wondrous sort of way.

"The magic is drawing it from you," Vale supplies.

"But Cyllian said there wasn't a cure for me."

"Then, your healer was wrong."

"Obviously," both Kristal and Nefari say. They share a grin with each other. It's the first time Cyllian has ever been wrong, but then again, the discovery of inferaze is fairly new to the Rebel Legion. Cyllian wouldn't have known any different than what she's been taught.

"Sibyl thought the sword was meant for Hope—or the Hope-favored," Nefari cautiously announces. She peeks at Vale, but only for a moment. "Is it true," she asks Kristal. "Does the Queen of Salix have captives she's using to lure the Hope-favored?"

"I've heard the rumors, too." Kristal pauses as she steers around a small boulder. "But I've never seen the captives myself. The queen is many things, and I have no doubt there are captives held in the dungeons, but I've never actually *seen* her captives, let alone know if this particular rumor is true. I tried not to think about what was below the main castle."

Sibyl was right, Nefari thinks to herself. There're many moving pieces, and what if one of those pieces happens to be the Queen of Salix holding Amoon as a prize to attract the Hope-favored . . .

Anger curls in Nefari's gut, but she hides it by saying, "If the inferaze can kill dark magic like the wraiths, then perhaps . . ."

"What?" Kristal chortles, but there's no humor in it. "You think my illness is dark magic?"

Nefari shrugs. "I think your illness is anything but ordinary, which might be why you and the sword are drawn to each other."

"Do I look like I'm infected with dark magic?" It was said as a genuine question, and Nefari thinks about how to soften her next words.

"Maybe it's not dark magic, but you were born in a castle filled with it. Still, as I said, it's not normal."

"Nothing is normal when it comes to me," she whispers.

"What's it like?" Vale inquires tentatively. "The castle, I mean. What's it like to live there?"

She doesn't look at him as she answers, "Dark. Brutal. The city is full of poverty, and the queen does not care."

"Would you do something about it if you could?"

"The best thing I could do is run, so at this moment, I would say no. I'm never going back. I'd rather die."

Near silence falls between them throughout the next few days, and when they finally reach the area safe enough to shadow jump, Nefari pauses and stares at all of the shadows before her, ready to be used. She swears they vibrate with anticipation, waiting to take her home.

Vale comes up beside her and places a hand on her shoulder. "What is it?" His tone is firm, and though she knows he hasn't shadow jumped either for fear of the wraiths, he shows no outward signs of nervous energy. It makes her mad, but she doesn't comment on the matter.

She blinks at her chosen shadow, so deeply dark it's like a void - a pocket of night absent stars. "We didn't run into a single crone."

"You wanted to?"

"I expected to." She turns to face him. "Something doesn't feel right, Vale."

Kristal fidgets beside them, peering all around. They pay her no mind. The more they traveled into the dangerous forest, the more frightened she became.

Gaze boring into hers, he asks, "Did you expect this to?"

She blows out a breath and scratches at an invisible itch along her neck. "I thought it would feel different. Perhaps, I wished it would feel like coming home, but it doesn't. Not a single crone, Vale. Not another single

86

creature. Not even Diabolus Beetle harvesters. There's been no one."

He squeezes her shoulder. "Take it as a blessing."

"Let's go retrieve the crown and get the hell out of here," Kristal murmurs, rubbing at her arm with her free hand.

CHAPTER EIGHT

Sibyl Withervein stands at the edge of her cave, watching the snowfall onto Kadoka City. The flap of wings pulls her attention away to the bone crier flying in her direction. Her heart hammers in her chest, and when the bird lands on the pommel of her bone centaur's sword, it caws, dropping a black stone from its beak. She snatches it before it can clatter to the ground.

As soon as her palm wraps around the soft stone, a vision takes hold, magic solely different than her own foresight.

Through another's eyes, she sees a person's reflection in a sheet of glass. No. Not glass. *Ice.* This person whose eyes she borrows is staring straight into the reflection, breath misting in frigid temperatures. It's old magic, dark magic. Magic she has yet to master.

High fog floats around this female stranger, and Sibyl knows that whoever this is, she's in the Frozen Fade, a place that calls to Sibyl on a biological level. It is clear that this woman is a young crone but slightly older than Sibyl, having grown into her woman's body.

Her bright blue eyes stare beseechingly back at Sibyl, and Sibyl dives deeper into the vision.

Sibyl takes a moment to memorize her appearance. A scar is slashed across her cheek, making one eye appear milkier than the other. Full lips complete her slender, heart-shaped face, and her blonde hair is tied back into a neat knot.

"Cousin," the woman speaks urgently then quickly peers at her surroundings and the giant grey wolf that sits behind her, waiting obediently. Sibyl has never seen a tamed wolf before. "My name is Sindray Withervein. I am Raygelle's only daughter, and by contacting you, I am breaking every faction rule."

Sibyl nearly hisses like an angry cat. Trouble. This woman was trouble, and she wants nothing to do with it. How did this 'Sindray' find her? How did she know Sibyl existed?

"What do you want?" Sibyl asks aloud, but the voice does not answer. This is a message and not a live connection.

"I don't have much time. Here, please see what I have seen." The woman presses her palm to the icy reflection, and the vision shifts entirely.

In the middle of a crone faction's camp, jutting ice shoots toward the skies. The ice has many doors, homes to the crones of whatever faction this is.

Crones, haggish women intermixed with a Salix army, are gathered in a circle around a fire in broad daylight. When the vision's eyes settle on Wrenchel Withervein, Sibyl sucks in a quick breath. She's squatting on a log around a fire with her sisters, a mischievous grin exposing her jagged black and yellow teeth.

"Our girls have sent word," Wrenchel says, her voice raspy and snake-like. "The princess of the Shadow Kingdom travels through the Shadled as we speak, but she does not travel alone. She is with two others, one being -" the second vision cuts off and returns to Sindray Withervein.

Her shoulders rise and fall as if labored by simply breathing. "I am sorry; I cannot hold on for much longer. This - it is exhausting magic, as I am sure you know."

Sibyl doesn't. She's never tried it. She doesn't even know how.

"What is happening?" Sibyl demands, forgetting this is only a message.

"There are two things you must be aware of. Beware that the crones know who she is. The Salix soldiers here - they say - beware of the Salix traveler who -" the vision fizzes until it cuts off entirely.

Enraged, Sibyl slams her fist into the centaur's boney leg.

"Beware of who!" Sibyl hollers to the open, cold air.

Fear curdles in her gut, and she turns back to her cave's entrance and scuttles past the skulls and paintings lining the wall. When she reaches her dome-shaped room, she hurries to her divine table. She quickly seats herself and, thinking about Sindray, she touches the skull.

The skull gasps, and in Sindray's voice, it says, "Born to have a heart as black as coal, the Choice-chosen's purity will have unending pull. A heart so gold is foretold, hidden in places where there's nothing but cold. She will be the sympathizer of both the enemy and kin, a shield for those shackled and sold. And with the wolf as a guide, she will choose to stand by those who wish they had died."

"Cousin. Sympathizer. Wolf." Sibyl glances at the torches still lit along the walls throughout her room. "Sindray is Choice-chosen."

And isn't that a dangerous game, a bright Divine in the company of dark creatures?

On a ship, Dao Pyreswift gazes in the direction of the Shadled Forest, it's purple leaves little dots on the horizon as he wonders how Nefari is fairing. The sea sprays his face, a warm and comfortable mist that coats every inch of his exposed skin.

They had stopped at a village by the Divine Bay's shore to board their horses and shop their markets for leather that would protect against the sea's harsh elements.

Now, Dao understands why.

They've set sail across the Divine Bay and straight for Hope's Island an hour ago. On the journey here, he'd managed to sleep little on the back of his horse, and neither had the others.

On the front of the ship, Dao, Fawn, Kaymen, and Cyllian watch the disappearing shore together. Dark purple splotches have formed under Fawn's eyes, but she refuses to show mercy, to show weakness when surrounded by Savage's criminals. She hadn't slept at all, for there was no carriage she could have fit into. Even on the ship, she's the largest on board. It'll be a difficult journey for her, but if Dao has learned anything over the past ten years, it is that centaurs adapt. Fawn is no exception. She's as stubborn as a mule.

Dao turns and leans his back against the rail to gaze out at the ship's deck and the endless bay beyond.

The crew Savage acquired was of no one Dao recognized - nameless sinners with missing teeth and ragged appearances, paid for by Bastian's good coin.

Savage is barking orders, occasionally falling into the old Pirate King demeanor like he'd never been tossed out of the title, pirate lilt and all.

"On the plus side, they're the only pirates we'll run into," Kaymen mutters.

Indeed, they would be the only, but at least they're leaving Dao's group alone. The usual pirates don't often sail around Loess and Sutherland to get to the Divine Bay and its islands. Most of the treasure from the islands have been pilfered already, except the inferaze. Until the Rebel Legion's discovery, no one knows the capabilities of the rock, though Dao is starting to wonder what Savage thinks.

There's a crew member who doesn't belong with the criminals, however. He sticks out among them, gentle and soft and kind-hearted. He's currently on deck, leaning against the rail, his eyes closed as he basks in the salt of the bay.

"Who is he, anyway," Dao asks Kaymen. The others turn and follow his line of sight to the brown-haired man with milky eyes.

"They call him Dyson," Fawn whispers. "I had already inquired about him because he doesn't seem . . . Savage's usual sort."

"And who is he rumored to be?" Dao is aware that almost everybody surrounded by Savage has some sort of rumor, often based in truth, and often more harrowing than the last.

"The elusive merchant who sold the inferaze in the Black Market," Cyllian mutters.

Dao looks at her, taking in her leather vest and leather pants swapped out from the usual healer's dress. He hasn't overlooked how striking she appears in them. Her braided hair flaps in the breeze like the white sails above them. "The one who Fari bought her blade from?" She nods, and he blows out a breath. "So we'll have to share our inferaze with another."

"I don't like the sound of that," Kaymen admits.

Dao peers at the man again. He's turned and staring directly at them. He lifts a hand and waves. "I don't think you'll need to be worried about him. It's Savage who has me worried."

"You think he'll double-cross us?" Fawn wonders aloud. She crosses her arms over her chest, defensive at just the mention of trouble.

"I think Savage isn't in this to fulfill a bargain." Dao stops talking because Dyson, the merchant, is climbing the stairs and approaching at a slow and cautious speed. Dao blinks at the man's eyes, questioning if he's blind. When he's closer, Dao swears the milky whites stir like fog and sparkle like Fari's sword.

It's an oddity, but the realm is full of that.

The merchant grins. "What are our chances of running into a pyren?"

"The alluring women with fins who can swim through any body of water?" Dao asks, saying the words quickly. He's heard the rumors about them. Has read about them. They come from the Demon Realm and often bring back half-dead sailors and unfortunate souls to their fee ruler. Though, now that the old fee are dead and the new ones have taken over . . . He isn't sure about the particulars anymore. He isn't sure where they side and how they behave. Only the pirates claim to have seen the pyrens in twenty years, and their word isn't gold.

"That's the one." Dyson scrubs at the brown, unruly stubble along his jaw. "I haven't seen one in what feels like ages."

"It sounds like you *want* to see one." Kaymen shifts his weight and puffs out his chest. "I don't think it wise."

"Misunderstood creatures." Dyson waves a hand in the air. "Harmless beasts if you know how to talk to them. If you know what to give them, and if you know how to avoid their lure, anyway."

"Ha," Kaymen adds without humor. "If you say so."

"I do. Savage, on the other hand," Dyson turns to study the crew with them, "you should watch what you say and do around him."

"We know," Fawn responds.

Dao wonders what this man could possibly know about creatures of water and men like Savage. Then again, Dyson has traveled these waters before and probably not by himself. Did Savage take him the first time? What does Savage think now, now that two are after the inferaze? The thought does not comfort him.

Cyllian's soft voice soothes Fawn's brash tone. "What do you know about him, Dyson?"

Dyson exhales slowly. "I imagine everything you do. They say he used to be the Pirate King?" They nod, and he continues, "When his daughter threw him overboard, how did he survive the water with only one good leg? Pyrens?"

Dao would love to know why he's so fascinated with water demons who could kill them or take down their ship in a heartbeat. They'd either be drowned, eaten, or become demons themselves. "That's a rumor that's only been speculated on."

"So are free shadow people, yet here you stand." Dyson quirks an eyebrow.

Huffing, Kaymen pushes past them, saying as he does, "Just don't go calling the pyrens during our journey. Do it on your own time. I have no desire to be their evening meal."

Dao couldn't agree more.

An hour later, Dao practices knife throwing with Fawn. Their knives hurtle through the air and embed into a shield strapped to the tall and thick wooden mast.

"When did you become so lax on your training," Fawn barks. He had missed, yet again, and this time, one of the crew curses as the knife shoots past the shield and into the rail right next to his hand. "Surely, your history books told you about the many wars over the centuries. A sword in your hand and sweat on your brow is prudent."

Grumbling under his breath, Dao crosses the deck to retrieve the dagger. *History is what keeps the future alive,* he doesn't say because he knows knowledge is as good as any blade. Fawn would never understand.

As soon as his hand wraps around the hilt, another dagger flies through the air, cuts through his shirt, and slices his arm. The dagger then embeds into the rail, right next to his own.

Clutching his fresh and deep wound, he whirls to face Fawn. Fawn has a smirk plastered on her face, and his cheeks redden in a blush. "What was that for?"

"Because you've become soft." She crosses her arms. "All those books have *made* you soft. They've made you question the skills I know you've been taught because I taught you them."

He digs both daggers out of the wood, blood dribbling down his arm and soaking his tunic's sleeve. "The comparison is not fair when I'm standing side by side with a weapon's master. You eat your breakfast with knives such as these." There's no truth to the words, but the impact is just the same.

He hands her back both daggers as she chortles. "Go see Cyllian before you bleed all over the deck. She and Kaymen are below."

Dao grumbles some more as he does what she says, passing Savage and Dyson deep in heated conversation along the way. His feet thunder down the steps and into the bowels of the boat, and there, seated at one of the few dining tables, are Cyllian and Kaymen. Neither is saying anything to one another, preferring the silence and the lap of water against the side of the ship while they play with a deck of cards.

Cyllian lays down her cards with a smirk. "I win again," she boasts.

Kaymen chucks his own cards onto the table. "Why can't I beat you?"

Collecting the cards, she stacks them into a neat pile. "Ah, don't be a sore loser. There are other players aboard the ship that you can surely best."

At his approach, both look up. Kaymen's eyes glitter with glee when he notices the wound, but Cyllian's take on a concerned edge.

He sits down next to Cyllian and huffs his annoyance.

"What happened?" She tears the cloth of his tunic to get a better look and probes the outer edges of the wound with a finger.

"Fawn," he grumbles, and that's all that needs to be said.

Kaymen stands and, upon passing, pats Dao on the shoulder. "She can be relentless. Don't let it wound your pride along with your arm."

Cyllian snorts as Kaymen climbs the steps to the deck. "Let me grab my things," she says, hustling away from the table and to the sleeping quarters of the ship. She returns not a minute later and sprawls her materials across the table. "How did this happen?"

Dao explains and then adds, "It's nothing. Just a scratch."

"It's deep," she corrects, examining it closer. She grabs cotton and wipes away the blood. He hisses when she dabs it with potent alcohol. Dao isn't surprised she had found some. The crew loves their spirits, having learned so along the way to the bay.

She grabs the needle and threads it. "This will sting," she warns.

"Do it."

She hisses with him at the first thread. "It could have been worse," he mumbles with a painfilled tone because her stiff posture tells him she's upset on the matter. "It was only a joke."

"It's better than the last scar Fawn gave you. What? Three years ago?" she touches the scar just below his wound then pokes it with her nail. "But you held up well with that one, as well."

Indeed, Kaymen hadn't always been Fawn's sparring partner. Dao used to be subjected to her pent-up wrath, but even Dao knows Fawn had always held back her true potential. Centaurs were quick, relentless, and strong. At least she had used a normal-sized blade instead of the centaur-sized.

He chuckles under his breath. "You stitched me up then, too." She meets his gaze. "If I remember correctly, I had loaned you a few of Swen's books on ancient healing remedies that day as payment for my misfortune."

She giggles and adds another stitch without looking. "Oh, to be young and so ignorant. The books helped me be the healer I am today, and for that, I'll always owe you a debt."

Warmth blossoms around Dao's heart. He quiets his voice, and he doesn't know why his tone takes on a purr-like quality, but he says, "I never saw those books again. What did you ever do with them?

A blush rises to her cheeks. "They're still in my room in the city's healer's hut. They're my most cherished possessions, you know."

He blinks. "Why? You know all the knowledge by now. Why do you still want to hold onto them?"

She returns her attention to the matter at hand, hesitating in answer. "It's not that I want to hold on to them for knowledge but rather because of who gave them to me."

She peeks up at him, and Dao swallows thickly.

CHAPTER NINE

Patrix Eiling sits below deck with Emory and the others, eating their measly afternoon meal as their ship sails for Loess, a place he'd rather not be going. It reeks of fish guts in the meager crew's living quarters, but it could be worse. They could be encountering the great water beast and have a whole host of new issues.

He chews on his bread in silence, letting Emory's voice fall over him like water on a cliff. Since they started this journey, Emory hasn't once shut his trap, except when his eyes were closed, but Patrix had learned how to tune him out after day one.

Youth, Patrix thinks. *They're so quick to blubber.*

It is a miracle that no one on board recognizes either Emory or Patrix. If they had, they sure haven't said anything, but then again, none have approached him to hold more than a one-sentence conversation. Patrix likes it like that, likes to be faceless and nameless and recognized as nothing but an ordinary citizen who doesn't hold the realm's secrets.

To their right, down the table, a woman sits. Daintily, she eats her meal, paying no mind to those around her rising from their cots to find their breakfast meal. Patrix has kept his eye on her ever since they left Widow's Bay. Not because she looks like trouble but because she's a satyr with striking beauty. She, too, had paid her way on for transportation.

Patrix studies her discreetly and the way her tight leathers fit her ample body. Her short white and bluish hair falls in waves around her head, framing her delicate jaw. Her square-shaped face brings out her full red lips, and it makes his body stiffen. She's not a pirate, nor does she belong to Urbana if her delicate horns are anything to go by. *Loess.* As a satyr, she's most likely from Loess, and she couldn't be much younger than him.

His thoughts often drift back to her even when he sleeps, but he has yet to say two words to her, aside from "Good morning," and "Thank you." He plans to rectify that immediately. Patrix isn't one to wait to grab what he wants, including but not limited to the Diablous Beetle powder he has stored in his pack that's hidden in his and Emory's paid-for chamber. He had bought it in the Black Market, Emory none-the-wiser while he paid the fee to travel on the boat.

Squinting with wicked intent, Patrix picks up his plate. Emory falls silent. "Where are you going?" he eventually inquires.

Patrix doesn't answer. He stands and moves to the end of the table until he's seated across from the vanilla-scented woman. She spies him suspiciously with forest-green eyes and sips from her milk in her horn mug.

"Do you ever wonder why we drink the breast milk from another animal?" Patrix asks. The words had just spilled out of him before he thought them over, and now he mentally kicks himself.

Brilliant, old boy. Brilliant, he chastises himself. *You're losing your touch, and you'll be lucky she doesn't smack you for it.*

She sets her cup down without the frown he expected. "Is that your best pick-up line, or are there more impressive others?" Her voice is like honey, and it slithers over Patrix in delightful ways.

"Today, it is. I'm Patrix." He purposefully omits his last name.

"Yayla Misleigh."

He settles better into his seat, pleased with himself. "And from where do you hail, Yayla Misleigh?"

She tears off a chunk of bread and pops it into her mouth while she narrows her eyes and considers him.

When she swallows, Patrix follows her throat's movements. "I imagine the same place you do."

Patrix chortles. "I may have been born in Loess, but that is not my home. It hasn't been for many years." Patrix doesn't know why he tells her the truth. The truth never spills from his own mouth, but there's something alluring about this woman who causes him not to think properly.

"Interesting," she responds disinterestedly. "So then, why are you sailing to Loess?"

He blows out a breath, meal forgotten. "Truth be told, I'm not sure anymore."

"Interesting," she voices again.

"Is that all you have to say?"

"Well, yes, when I know who I'm speaking to."

He quirks a brow, but his blood runs cold just the same. "And who do you think you're speaking to?"

"Why, the spy of many kingdoms and a womanizer to boot." The words are mocking, and he would normally find them concerning had she not known who he truly was.

A blush rises to his cheeks, staining them with heat. He puts his elbows on the table and steeples his fingers in front of his mouth to hide the grin he fakes. "I don't suppose you'd want to oblige the latter rumor?"

105

She returns the grin. "Absolutely not." And with that, she gets up and walks away, leaving her plate for Patrix to take care of. He watches her hips sway as she climbs the stairs and disappears onto the sunny deck.

Emory scoots to sit beside him. "That was the worst let-down I've ever seen, especially for you."

"Sassy," Patrix says distractedly. "I like sassy."

"I don't think she liked you," Emory interjects with a poke to his friend's ribs.

"Oh," he counters, drawing out the word. "I think she does."

Emory scowls. "I don't think you should be starting anything with anyone. I told Dao we'd try to get the Queen of Loess, your aunt, to side with the Legion. I don't think this was part of my rewardless bargain."

He slaps Emory on the shoulder and rises. "I can do both, Young Lad. I can do both." He makes his way up the stairs with every intention of watching Yayla from afar.

In her shadow people form, Nefari and Vale stare at what was once their home. The only thing that remains the same is the star-speckled sky. The sky hugs the kingdom tightly, shimmering with shades of blue and purple. Matching purple, blue, and green cobblestones stretch out from under their feet and sprawl in every direction, leading to what were once teaming homes, prosperous shops, and large stables with finely bred horses of plenty. Those horses were traded with Sutherland, but now, the silence stretches taut without the sounds of their whinnies and the voices of many.

Most of the cobblestones no longer rest evenly. Instead, it's as though an earthquake shook the kingdom and rattled the stones. The stones shift under their steps, making balance awkward.

She touches her lip as she takes it all in, allows it to harden her heart for her mission to come.

Most of the shops are still intact, but others, closer to the castle, are in rubble or ash. She remembers this area smelling of candies and flowers and clothing dye, but now the aroma of dust permeates the air.

Nefari curls her fingers into a fist, feeling her ring biting into her palm. Even the florist, her favorite shop, is a collapsed heap with beams jutting up like arrows to a fallen giant's back.

"Wow," Kristal whispers in awe. "It's a garden of shadows, twilight, and death." Her gaze wanders around the market, taking in the kingdom stuck between day and night. Things shimmer while others glitter as though their objects and bricks and straw roofs are speckled with faded stars.

Kristal takes in the overgrown gardens and the weeds cracking between the cobbles. Bones are carelessly thrown about from a blast of magic ten years ago. Femurs and skulls and hands and . . .

On numb feet, Nefari leads them down the path, stepping over or weaving around the debris from the fallen shops and their wares.

Ahead, the small castle gleams. "How is it still standing?" Nefari asks in a whisper. She doesn't expect an answer because, truth be told, she hadn't meant to say it aloud.

The sense of home and the familiar smells she hadn't remembered until now fog her brain and coherent thoughts. These emotions make her feel a sense of belonging, and also a sense of foreboding, a war between her memories and heart. She had imagined what this place would look like after her mother's blast, but she hadn't expected . . . *this*. Not really.

Their feet echo against the cobbles as Vale scrubs his jaw, wary of the absolute silence of the kingdom. "Perhaps it was sturdy enough to withstand a royal's magic. It's made of the toughest brick after all."

The closer they get to the castle, the more bones they see. Skulls squat along the streets, overtaken by growing vegetation. Dotted here and there are shadow roses, black flowers which sparkle like the night sky. They grow along tipped over decaying fences, and the vines stretching up one side of the castle's wall have grown wild, overtaking much of one side of the castle.

"This is beautiful," Kristal proclaims, ignoring the emotions of Vale and Nefari that are rising to unbearable grief. She bends to smell the roses and sighs contently. "You lived here?"

"We were born here," he corrects with distaste. He still hasn't warmed to Nefari's friend, and with a sigh, Nefari wonders if he ever will. Is it just Kristal and where she was born, or is it the fact that she's Nefari's friend? She hasn't figured out which, but she has perceived a sense of possession over the last few days. She isn't sure how to rectify it, how to insert a bond between the two that's somewhat more comfortable than this.

A tender breeze urges Nefari closer and closer to the castle, and she swears, for a heartbeat, she hears her mother's voice in it. "Be brave," the voice says. She allows it to seep in and calm her nerves.

"Are you ready?" Vale studies her when they pass the mess of a courtyard and reach the castle doors.

"No," she answers truthfully, but she wraps her hand around the brass knob anyway, and pulls.

A stale gust brushes against her nose, full of dust. They step into its dark entrance.

They wander through the castle, ignoring all of the bones and Kristal's wandering gaze as they travel through dark hallways, completely ignoring the entrance to the throne room entirely. Grit grinds beneath their boots as they pass. Nefari is thankful the doors are shut because she doesn't think she could handle stepping on the ash of her people. That was where her mother released the blast, saving who she could by death or escape.

The closer they get to her mother and father's chambers, the more she smells her mother's scent. It lingers here like the smell of flowers on a hot summer day.

When they pass one particular room, Nefari pauses by the doorway. Rubble is all that remains inside. The vanity is in splinters, and the bed's sheep-fluff is tossed about with the cobwebs and tumbling balls of dust.

"What was this place?" Kristal inquires softly when she doesn't move.

"The princess's bedroom," Vale supplies, staring at the entrance to her closet. It was where they had hidden when they heard screams, but all Nefari can look at is the brown stain of what was Amoon's blood, spread out in what used to be a puddle. There's so much of it she's surprised Amoon survived.

Nefari closes down her mind when she thinks about what Amoon must look like now. The thought was as painful as the throne room.

"You knew the princess?"

"You could say that," she answers, her voice cracking.

"And is that where she died?" she asks, pointing to the dried puddle. She doesn't get an answer. Kristal, taking it as a confirmation, places a comforting hand on her shoulder and gently squeezes. "I didn't know. And for what it's worth, I'm sorry for your loss."

Nefari nods. Tears spring to her eyes when Vale leads them away. It's a chapter of her life she's not sure if she's ready to close or not.

They reach her parent's chambers in what feels like seconds. What will they see inside? Will there be the blood of the servants? Destruction like her own room? She's not ready. She's not ready to have whatever is inside a taint on her already bruised soul.

"Breathe, Fari," he whispers in her ear, a comforting arm around her. "You must breathe, or we will not get through this."

She swallows, blows out a breath, and says, "Okay," shoving her feelings down, down, down until they're only a kernel of grief.

He pushes the door open, and she gasps.

CHAPTER TEN

"Why isn't this place destroyed, too?" Kristal bluntly asks.

Everything inside is untouched like the room was warded from the blast itself. The bed is made. The logs by the fireplace are neatly piled, and the fur draped over the two high back chairs is still wrinkle and dust-free. There are no cobwebs, no tumbling dust balls . . .

It's as though it's still lived in, though she knows otherwise. They haven't encountered a living being since the beast in the Shadled.

Nefari steps inside, holding her breath for a second as she beats back the returning emotions. "I don't know. Was it protected somehow?"

"Perhaps. That explains why they always knew we were playing in here or inside the tunnel," Vale grumbles.

"Or," Nefari counters. "They knew because they're parents and nothing more. Your own father was often the one who caught us. As children, we weren't exactly stealthy."

"True."

"You two played in the castle?"

Vale stiffens beside Nefari. "Something like that."

"Vale," Nefari calls solemnly. They can't complete this without telling her because, in order to gain entrance into the tunnel, they'll need Nefari's blood - the blood of an heir. The blood of a royal. And if they are to explain how and where she knows the crown might be . . .

Kristal will have questions, questions Nefari has no desire to continue to lie about. Not when Kristal has been truthful and trusting thus far.

"No," he barks when he sees all of these thoughts playing across her face. "Don't you dare."

"Don't what?" Kristal looks back and forth between the two.

Nefari turns to her, her back to Vale. "I'm not who I said I was. I am not who you think I am."

He steps up beside her beseechingly. "Nefari, don't!"

She waves him off with a quick swipe through the air, and as she does, she spots a familiar object on her

113

father's nightstand. She travels to it and touches the yarn hair of the doll Beau Timida had made her while memories crash back like the weight of a crumbling wall.

"Who are you, then?" Kristal cocks her head to the side and studies her up and down.

She turns back to the group, doll in hand. "I didn't just play here. I lived here."

Kristal's eyebrows pull together. "As a servant?"

She brushes the doll's hair with her fingers. "No. Not a servant."

Her eyes widen as she takes Nefari in once more. "You're . . . you're her! You're - you're -" she backs away and bumps into one of the high-backed chairs. "You look just like your mother. You're - you're the heir! The dead princess!"

"I am," Nefari whispers. She places the doll perfectly back on the nightstand. The action is like a final rest to her unrest. At that moment, warmth swirls inside her. Warmth at finally admitting to who and what she is. Admitting to someone who is supposed to be her enemy and instead became her great friend. Kristal was someone who saved her life when she didn't have to and at the expense of herself.

She didn't want to be a liar, nor did she want to continue to lie to herself. "I am the princess said to be dead, and that is not my blood on the floor of my old bedroom."

"You're supposed to be dead!" she shouts unhelpfully. It echoes throughout the room. "The princess died ten years ago."

"The princess did die ten years ago," Nefari continues, still whispering. "I am not the same girl I was when everyone - when the Harvest Storm raided my home."

"She is the Queen of the Shadow People," Vale claims in a clear tone, unaffected by the title as Nefari is. Nefari looks at him, noting the steel edge of his set jaw.

Kristal covers her mouth as tears spring to her eyes. She shifts her attention to the arching windows overlooking the courtyard. "You lied to me."

A blush rises to Nefari's cheeks, but she crosses the distance just the same. "I wanted to tell you for the entire journey, but I didn't know where to begin."

Kristal snaps her attention back to them. "You could have started with the truth! And who are you?" she demands of Vale. "Were you really her intended?"

"Yes, and as for your first statement, you were the enemy," Vale supplies. "She didn't have to tell you anything, and in my opinion, she shouldn't have told you now."

A pause pulls the room tight, and just for a moment, she hears her mother say, "Be brave," again. Nefari looks to both of them, but they hadn't seemed to have heard it.

"I deserved to know," Kristal murmurs, the fight leaving her voice.

Nefari places her hands on Kristal's shoulders. She catches her eyes and says, "I wanted to tell you. You have to believe me. It just wasn't safe for anyone. Please. Please try to understand."

Kristal's throat bobs as she swallows and lowers her hand. "I do understand, but right now . . ."

Pulling her into a hug, Nefari adds, "I broke your trust. I know. And for that, I am sorry."

Nefari wonders if, had Patrix apologized, she would have softened toward his plight as well.

They linger there for a moment, hugging each other while allowing Kristal to accept the truth until Vale interrupts the moment with a clearing of his throat. "Are we going to find the crown, or are we going to continue . . . whatever *this* is."

Nefari licks her lips to hide her smirk, then pulls away. She pats Kristal's cheek and comments, "The crown is this way." She tips her head to the side, indicating to the sealed tunnel, and then turns to face it herself.

"I don't see anything," Kristal vows because, unless one knows where to look, it appears as nothing but a wall. Then, out loud, she reads the passage carved out above the door. "Darkness cannot dwell where there is light."

"My mother used to say that all the time. Her magic, like mine, was starlight - bright and blinding and hot."

Kristal exhales. "Your mother, the queen, the savior . . ." Nefari and Vale both look at her. "What? It's going to take some getting used to. At least, I know why your hair was darker in your human form," she mutters, her last sentence said grudgingly.

Without another word, Nefari pulls a dagger from her hip, shuffles past the bed, and approaches the wall.

"What are you doing?" Kristal's accent is thick.

"The blood of my blood sealed this door, and the blood of my blood will open it." As children, it hadn't taken much to figure it out.

"It's like deja vu," Vale says beside her. He takes the knife from her palm and asks, "Like old times?"

Biting her bottom lip, Nefari nods.

"Don't wince," he adds with a wink then draws the blade across her palm.

Nefari does wince, but blood immediately wells and pools in the cup of her palm. The wound isn't deep, but

117

it's enough for their purpose. He takes her hand and presses it to the small section of the wall that's carved with a cluster of stars. It's a practice both she and Vale remember with perfect clarity. Perhaps the wounds on her hand are how her parents knew they'd been with the treasures and not some silly preserving magic.

The door groans and jerks then slides open, revealing a dark and dusty stairwell leading to the treasures of the Shadow Kingdom.

Vale tears a part of his tunic and hands it to Nefari. She wraps it around the wound and ties a knot using her teeth.

Blowing out a breath, Vale travels to the torch along the wall and sparks it to life with flint from his cloak pocket. He picks up the torch, and with one last look at Nefari, he dips inside.

Nefari follows close behind, Kristal on her heels.

"Watch your step," Vale cautions. "The stairs are slick. You'll be sliding around like a pig on ice if you're not careful."

Indeed, the steps were damp and full of mildew. They tread carefully, feet echoing with every step. Nefari nearly jumps out of her skin when Kristal sneezes, however. She glares over her shoulder at her friend, but Kristal pays her no mind.

"This doesn't look ominous or anything," Kristal mutters.

"It's been sealed," Nefari divulges with little patience. "No dark beast will be crawling within unless my mother had hidden one for all these years, and even then, we'd only find its bones."

Under the weight of what's to come, the shadows bend and crawl toward her upon their descent. Instead of frightening her, they calm her further.

"That explains everything," Kristal expresses, commenting on it with a sliver of fear in her tone. "That night - the Shadow Mourn Eve - I swore I saw the same thing. The shadows seem to breathe for you."

"They do," Nefari murmurs. "I'm Fate-favored and the Queen of the Shadows."

"Does this mean you can do more magic than stars?"

"Yes, but I don't know exactly -"

Kristal gasps. "You can't. You can't do magic because of the wraiths."

"If you two are done gossiping," Vale says at the bottom of the stairs, "we have some hunting to do."

All around them lay treasures upon treasures, and they glint in Vale's light.

"Oh, my Divine," Kristal breathes. "The Pirate Queen would die."

Piles of gold squat in a shadow to the left, shimmering their reflections. Old antique pictures rest against the wall to their left, some torn and some still intact. Silver and gold armor, swords, and shields. There are vases of many shapes and sizes, wedding dresses jeweled with diamonds, and three chests of blue, purple, and yellow jewels lining the far wall. In the middle chest, atop the jewels, is a crown, the crown she remembers so well.

The pieces of the crown are like vines that wind and weave around one another, and set into them are black jewels. They spark and sparkle like a galaxy.

Vale strides to the middle chest and plucks up the crown as if it were nothing but a large rock. He weighs it in his hand. "I never thought I'd see this again." He makes his way back to Nefari and holds it out for her to take. "It's missing a jewel, though."

"Marred perfection," Kristal barks, defending Nefari and her family's heirloom. "Try it on."

With shaky fingers, Nefari takes the crown from Vale. "I shouldn't."

"She's right." Vale squints at her. "It's yours. You should put it on if anything but for this moment until you can fully take back your kingdom."

With peer pressure weighing down her shoulders, she reluctantly obeys. Its heavy size settles on her head, and Vale and Kristal beam at her. She doesn't leave it on for long, though, because doing so . . . well, it isn't comfortable, both emotionally and physically.

Nefari hardly ever saw her mother wear it, and this was probably why. Did her mother ever feel like she stole the title from her parents?

She had never met her grandfather or grandmother. They were long dead when she came along, but she's seen pictures of them in the throne room. Had they felt the same way too? Was this a normal feeling? Nefari is not bound to know the answers.

"See?" Nefari says, removing the crown. "Nothing magical happened. They're hunting this thing for nothing."

"Well, it isn't nothing," Vale grumbles. "It's a trophy for them, a piece to hang over Amoon."

"Amoon?" Kristal cocks her head to the side.

"Our friend, the one who bled on my bedroom floor. She was captured as a child and has been in the Salix's dungeon for ten years."

"Oh." Kristal blushes, the action visible despite the dark. "Sorry. Is that the captive you spoke of?"

"Yes," Vale answers, the word a snip.

Nefari huffs. "You don't need to apologize for something you couldn't have controlled. You were a servant. You couldn't have done anything about what the Queen ordered done."

As it perches in her palm, Nefari stares at the crown while Kristal and Vale continue on a conversation about if she'll indeed take back her kingdom and how she might go about doing it. Nefari doesn't care. Balanced on her palm is a piece of her mother.

She rubs her finger over the hole where the stone would be nestled. "I wonder what happened to it," she interrupts them.

"Pardon?" Kristal asks.

"The stone. Where did it go?"

Dismissively, Vale remarks, "It's old, Fari. It probably broke off years ago."

Nefari hums. She hadn't noticed it when she was a child, but then again, her mother hardly ever let her pick it up.

Kristal scrutinizes it over her shoulder. "They look like little inferaze pieces."

"They do, and - " Nefari pauses, scowling. She rests the heavy crown in one hand while she lifts her other hand with the ring her mother gave her. She turns it to face Vale's torchlight and studies it. "No. No, it can't be . . ."

Vale squints at the ring, then the crown, flame flaring about his head. "It looks like it'd be a fit. Do you want to try it?"

Nodding, she holds out her hand. He passes the torch to Kristal and wiggles the ring free.

"Be careful," Kristal cautions.

He snaps an annoyed glance at her. He then takes Nefari's dagger, which, to her annoyance, he had kept, and pries the black diamond free.

"Be brave," Nefari whispers to herself while blowing out a breath. Neither had heard her.

She takes the diamond from Vale's hand and, with one last look at her companions, she inserts the diamond. It slides in easily, and right when she grasps the crown with two hands, the crown glows purple, similar to the way the northern lights shimmer above the Fades.

Kristal and Vale gasp, but Nefari blinks. The purple brightens the treasure room, and where the circlet is for the head of a queen, images begin to appear.

The first image is of Nefari, standing in the cave. A male voice speaks, and she steals a glance at Vale. It's not him. Is it the crown? Fate perhaps? She feels a familiar pull to the voice, an allure equivalent to kinship.

"She will shape the darkness," this voice says. "this Fate-blessed princess of rage and wrath, for she is the crown of endless night and the memory of woeful shadows. Echoes of clinking chain and metal, the sharp sting of leather. The hopeful shards of a broken kingdom will find the fated queen, and then, darkness will yawn and swallow the realm."

"That's you," Kristal mutters, but she clamps her mouth shut when the image shifts to the protruding ice of The Fades. A woman appears, a gentle-looking crone. Her yellow hair is tied neatly back, and a scar slashes across her eye down to her weak chin.

"Born to have a heart as black as coal, the Choice-chosen's purity will have unending pull. A heart so gold is foretold, hidden in places where there's nothing but cold. She will be the sympathizer of both the enemy and kin, a shield for those shackled and sold. And with the wolf as a guide, she will choose to stand by those who wish they had died."

"Is that Choice-chosen?" Kristal asks when the voice is finished, playing the woman walking among the crones. Nefari already knew the Choice-chosen was a crone, but never had she expected to be shown who it was.

The pirates were right. The Queen of Salix was right. The crown does show the Divine's whereabouts.

"It has to be," Nefari whispers.

Vale huffs as the image shifts once more.

"What is this?" Kristal questions because there, in the image, is Kristal, standing in the tunnel with Vale and Nefari. It circles around her body, displaying her shocked expression.

"In years of pain, the Hope-favored has been a silent witness to the darkness's violent reign. Both powerless and powerful, she will be the hope to the captives who cower. On her eighteenth birthday, she will rise with the very shadows she befriends and become the enemy of her own kin."

"My Divine." Nefari drops the crown.

CHAPTER ELEVEN

"You're her," Nefari whispers. The torchlight flares with shadows. "You're the Hope-favored."

"No." Kristal shakes her head. "No, I'm just a girl."

"No, you're not," Vale interjects. He swipes a hand over his mouth. "The illness. Its - It's-"

"You're not of magic," Nefari interjects. The color drains from her cheeks. "You're not *born* of magic. Your illness is your body's way of being overloaded by Hope's magic."

"And Hope's sword draws it away from you, giving you a reprieve." Vale laughs, but there's no humor in it. "Why didn't I see it before?"

"But I've never seen Hope!"

"I never saw Fate!" Nefari plucks the crown from the ground. "It did not lie! You are the Hope-favored!"

Vale begins to pace, ignoring them. "So, the true Divine Gods are really gone."

She covers her mouth once more. "What - What do I do? I don't have any magic."

"That you know of," Nefari spits.

Vale runs a hand through his long hair and turns to face them. "This changes everything. You'll have to discover whether you have magic, Salix Blood. You may not have any at all, except for the sword, which, I think I can speak for everyone when I say it belongs to you now."

Nefari scowls. "But it's my sword."

"Not anymore. Get over it." He shakes his head, long white hair spilling over a shoulder. "Fate has a funny way of doing things. You should know that better than anyone. It has a way of drawing connections. Your journey was to give it to her. 'Both powerless and powerful, she will be the hope to the captives who cower.'" He finger quotes the last sentence and looks Kristal in the eye. "You're from Salix. It would make sense that they're talking about the slaves there - our people."

Nodding absentmindedly, solely distracted, Kristal repeats the prophecy out loud. "I turn eighteen in less than two months' time. 'On her eighteenth birthday, she will rise with the very shadows she befriends and become the enemy of her own kin.' The shadows I befriend must mean you and the others of the Rebel Legion. But, I don't understand what I could possibly do. Rise and be the enemy to my kin? What does that even mean?"

"It means you have a part to play in all this," Vale grumbles, and Nefari gets the impression he wishes otherwise.

Dusk falls on the Divine Bay. Dao Pyerswift strides across the deck to where Fawn chats with one of the nameless males. Dao hasn't bothered to converse with any of the criminals on board, but Fawn has. She's always been sociable with the opposite sex.

Seawater laps the side of the ship while a chilly breeze comes off the water. Above them, the moon is a faded orb amid the purple sky, and one star twinkles brightly in the north. Dao peers at the star, but only for a moment.

They're already finished with Hope's Island, a mountainous and tropical green speck in the distance. The inferaze was found in the caves along the shore, and it hadn't taken much to find it - not near as long as it took to mine it. The rock is sturdy, and even though the caves were dark, the substance sparkled.

With a speculative expression, Savage had watched on from the entrance of the caves, not lifting a finger as his men, Dao's group, and Dyson chipped away at their bounty under the hot sun. He hadn't said a word either.

Now, having harvested the inferaze, they've stored it in large potato sacks and crates below deck where was once their dining tables. And even though everyone's mission is almost complete, he doesn't like the way they're looking at him today. He hasn't since Savage watched them mine the stuff.

He pulls Fawn aside, and he tells her as much. "Something's going on. Savage has been hulled up in his cabin all day with a few others, refusing an audience and doing the Divine knows what."

Fawn quirks a brow. "Perhaps he doesn't like you."

"I agree," a voice says behind them. Dyson has been a lingering, albeit mostly silent presence on board. "Savage doesn't like anyone, but this is highly unusual, and we should proceed with caution. Pirates are never quiet after pilfering an island, rocks or not."

Dao turns to him, including him in Fawn and his circle. "What do you suggest?"

"I -"

The cabin door creaks open and bangs against the damp wall. Savage's wooden leg thumps as he steps outside, a wicked grin on his face. Having emerged from the deck below, Kaymen and Cyllian join Dao, Dyson, and Fawn. "What's going on?" Cyllian asks, her tone soft and sweet as though she doesn't suspect the same things Dao does.

A wrong feeling settles over Dao. "Something isn't right," he whispers to them because that wicked gleam in Savage's expression is pinned on them. "I've read about this. I've read about what happens next in the pirate history books inside Swen's library."

"Of course, you have," Kaymen grumbles. "Do you mind sharing with the group?"

"Prepare yourselves," Dyson whispers.

"Ladies and gents," Savage calls to his crew. The three men inside the cabin step out with him, a solid wall of support from behind. Everyone stops their duties. Dao's group collectively sucks in a breath as Savage unsheathes his sword and points it at them from across the distance. "We have an unwanted company aboard who desires what's ours. If you so see fit, toss them overboard."

Dao, Kaymen, and Fawn draw their swords, and Dao tucks Cyllian behind him. "Stay," he demands of her.

"I can help!"

He peers over his shoulder, and his expression softens when he witnesses fear in her eyes. It wrenches unfamiliarly at his heart. "You have no weapons. Please, stay behind me."

"Are you prepared?" Dyson asks them, hands ringing at his sides.

"Spit it out, merchant." Kaymen crouches. "What's the plan?"

"What I do next . . . do *not* panic."

"Panic?" Cyllian is incredulous. She stands on her toes and surveys the scene from over Dao's shoulder.

"Do not panic," he repeats through his teeth.

"What are you going to do?" Kaymen whips his head to Dyson. "You're blind!"

Dao knows this isn't true. The man mined the inferaze without issue.

Dyson spares Kaymen a wicked gleam. "Whoever said I was blind?" Bending slightly, Dyson cups his hands and spins them in a circle. On the third spin, a sparkling white and lavender cloud forms between his palms, a close resemblance to his eyes. "Where I come from, the inferaze is plentiful, and it is different - works differently if one knows how to wield it."

"We have a magic wielder on board!" Savage announces, followed by a cackling chortle. "I knew there was something funny about you, boy. Are you a crone?"

"Not a crone." Dyson's jaw flexes as his magic grows in size and strength. It sounds like a gust of wind, though different from the gale of the sea. "A fee."

Dao double blinks. *A fee? They're . . . Oh, dear Divine.* They've been traveling with a legend of old! As a growing youth in the mountains, he had been fascinated with their history, their species, and how the Divine had made them to be what they are, remaking them when their children became unruly and greedy.

He should have known Dyson wasn't an ordinary man. He had seemed odd - off and different than all of the merchants Dao had ever come across.

But his milky eyes . . . His eyes telling of the pure magic within.

Kaymen curses while Savage's laugh increases in volume. "The fee are gone from this realm," Savage says. "Try again."

"Not this fee." Dyson's voice is deadly hushed but godlike in nature.

Savage nods to a group of criminals. They draw their swords without hesitation, and one rushes Dyson. Dyson hurls his magic at him, and the man hollers as he flies until his back hits the rail. He falls onto his knees, heaving to get his breath back.

"Call the pyrens!" Dyson shouts to them over his shoulder. He circles his hands again, and the magic cracks the space around them like static. "Call them now!"

"What?" Fawn demands while she watches the magic with uncertainty. "No!"

The fallen criminal gathers himself to his feet unsteadily.

"We're not calling them!" Kaymen exclaims.

Dyson curses and throws more magic at the group now running to them, swords poised. Their thunderous feet echo across the planks until they're swept out from under them.

"Get up, you fools!" Savage demands. He gestures with his free hand and a wave of his sword.

Shifting his stance slightly, Dyson peers back at them, his eyes glowing a white as bright as the prominent moon. "Drop your blood in the water, or so help me, I'll murder you myself!"

Without warning, Cyllian unstraps a short knife from Dao's leg, dashes to the ledge, and slits her hand with no hesitation. "Cyllian, don't!" Dao calls, but despite the growing darkness, he can clearly see her blood already dripping overboard and to the churning water below.

The entire crew rushes them. Dyson hurls magic at a few, and Dao raises his sword to prepare himself. His heart thunders in his ears as his sword collides with another.

Dao, despite a few years with a nose behind a book and his earlier mishap with Fawn, falls into the familiar ease of the dance between blades. It is like he never missed a day of practice. It is like he was born to protect the people he cares for.

He whirls, crouches, and parries the sword of the other man's while Fawn and Kaymen endure their own battle beside him.

Swords clash. Men and women grunt. More magic flashes to brighten the night, and soon, an all-out battle completely unfolds upon the deck.

With a stab to the gut, Dao cuts down the man who first approached him, and he kicks him to the rail. Cyllian cries out when the man tries to grab for her, but his grip slips on her tunic. He loses his balance and falls overboard. Water splashes below.

Dao rushes to the rail, and there, bobbing in the water, are a dozen emerald green pyrens of legend old. Their tentacle hair moves like individual octopus legs, and their sharp teeth gleam with wicked intent. They dive for the fallen man whose blood colors the water a purple-ish red.

A knife embeds itself in the rail, right by Dao's hand. Dao moves in front of Cyllian when a shout of anger follows the thud of the knife. He whirls to find Savage charging him, dashing past Dyson's defenses.

Dao raises his sword just in time. The strength in the blocked blow rings Dao's ears, and he grits his teeth to hold his own against the large and skilled pirate.

"Ye be fools if ya believe to survive this," Savage growls in his face, falling into the old pirate lilt like it's a familiar friend.

"You're a fool to believe we won't defend what's ours." No doubt, the pirate wants the inferaze to increase his status or return himself to his status among the pirate chain. Dao won't have it. "You can't have the inferaze, Deeds."

"It's mine. Everything on this ship is mine, includin' ya lives."

With a grunt and all of the strength he can muster against Savage's weight against his blade, Dao pushes him back and dances away. The wound along his arm from his time with Fawn pulls and tugs painfully, but he doesn't show mercy. He doesn't flinch away. He keeps his wits about him.

Savage comes at him time and time again, and Dao allows it, dodging, weaving, parring. Soon, sweat beads at Dao's temples. "You said you'd provide passage!"

A clash of swords. A ring of metal against metal. The sound of his heart in his ears.

"I said I'd get ya to Hope's Island. I said nothing about bringin' ya back."

Dao jumps out of the way of Savage's swipe and turns, and when Savage begins to breathe heavily, he strikes back. Blow after blow after blow, he pushes Savage toward the edge of the ship.

And when Savage's back bumps into the rail, cracking it, his balance swaying, Dao demands with his sword tucked under Savage's beard, "Give up, Savage, and I'll allow you to live. You don't have to die. Not here. Not today."

The ship rocks as the pyrens push, and Savage's sword clatters from his hands when his balance falters.

"I'll never give up!"

"So be it," Dao snarls. He lifts his leg and kicks Savage in the stomach. The rail breaks, and Savage falls overboard. He screams the whole way to the water and screams some more when the pyrens charge.

His screams are cut off when they pull him under.

Dao braces his free hand against the rail, taking deep inhales and slow exhales to catch his breath. His clothes cling to his wet skin, and the vein in his neck pulses heavily. *He's gone. Savage Deeds is dead* and by the hands of himself.

Breathing heavily, Dao turns back to the deck. Fawn pushes the last criminal to the same fate as Savage Deeds.

Cyllian runs to Dao's side and checks him for injuries as Dao takes in his group. Blood trickles down his arm as his eyes pin on Dyson. He leans against a barrel of ale, seemingly unaffected as he picks at his nails.

Sheathing his sword, Dao marches to him and shoves his shoulder. "Who the hell are you?"

CHAPTER TWELVE

"I told you not to panic," Dyson grumbles.

"You're a fee!" Kaymen shouts, touching the fresh but shallow cut on his cheek. "A gods forsaken fee!" He curses some more and flicks the blood from his fingertips.

"And yet, you're panicking." Dyson pushes off the barrel and crosses his arms. "My name is Dyson Coleman, Fee of the Dream Realm." His expression crumbles to a frown, and his milky eyes look beyond them. "Though I was once a wolf shifter on the Earth Realm, and then I was a rebellious shade on the Death Realm, then I was alive again . . . It's all very special. Truly fond memories." His sarcasm isn't missed, but everyone blinks dumbfoundedly at him anyway.

"Why are you here?" Fawn asks calmly as she sheaths her sword and adjusts her vest. She is without injuries, but that's no surprise to Dao.

She widens her stance to steady her balance against the still-rocking ship. "And where is your famed wolf?" They've all heard the legends about the big wolf who helps the Fee of the Dreams govern his realm.

"With the Choice-chosen." He splays open his arms and encompasses the realm. "I'm here to fight the good fight. And, to make sure the inferaze gets into the right hands."

"He fought Despair in the Tween," Dao grumbles to the group. The Tween is the space between life and death, a near realm all in itself if the legends are true. He had read about it when Swen made him learn the battle of the realms. It didn't take much for him to be fascinated by it. He read everything that had happened over two decades ago before he was even a twinkle in his mother's eye.

The group collectively sighs, but it's Cyllian who speaks. "What do we do now?"

"Now, I send the pyrens back to Aiden on the Demon Realm, and then you sail home with your burdens."

Relief floods through Dao. For a moment, he wasn't sure if Dyson would confiscate the inferaze and take it back to his realm. "What about you? Where will you go?"

"I'm going home. This realm may be beautiful, but it's full of dark and dangerous things. I've had enough of that for a lifetime. Several lifetimes." Dyson grins, travels to the rail, and whistles low. The ship stops rocking as the pyrens leave without a lyrical song, and he returns to them. "It's only temporary. I'll return when I'm needed again, and I probably won't be alone if I can talk the others into it. My wolf will stay here, however. His work is not done."

"What wolf?" Cyllian whispers. Her question goes unanswered.

"You're not going to help with Despair, are you," Kaymen grumbles. It wasn't a question.

"There's nothing to help with at this moment. This is up to you guys."

"Helpful," Fawn hisses. "So helpful."

Dao scowls. "Before you go . . ."

"Yes?" Dyson draws out the word.

"Why did you sell Nefari the sword she has?"

As if slapped, he juts his chin to the side. "To help her. She needed the strength, and someday, if not already, she will give the sword to the Hope-favored where it belongs."

"Nefari found the Hope-favored?" Dao asks in a breathless whisper.

There's a mischievous twinkle in Dyson's eyes, and without a word and a whoosh of his hands, he disappears in a cloud of sparkling smoke.

As soon as he's gone, Cyllian punches Dao's shoulder on the same arm his wound had reopened. Dao grabs his arm and barks, "Ouch!" Scowling, he whirls to face her. "What was that for?"

"I can take care of myself," she huffs.

"I was trying to protect you!"

Angrily, she grabs his arm and looks at the reopened wound. "And now you have gone and reopened the stitches."

The group falls away, manning the boat now that the crew is all but gone. Fawn takes charge as Kaymen grabs the wheel, steering the ship back on course.

Dao ignores it all as her anger toward him tugs at his heart.

"Cyllian," Dao whispers, taking her arm from her grasp and tipping her face to meet his. "I was trying to protect you. Nothing more, nothing less."

The rage sparking in her eyes dampens for a moment. "Just because I have become a healer doesn't mean I can't take care of myself. I still remember my lessons, Dao. I still know -"

"You stopped sparring the moment you became a healer."

"So did you when you picked up your first scroll! That doesn't mean I've forgotten anything." Her fingers curl into fists. "You sure haven't, keeping your nose stuffed behind a book."

He mockingly puts a hand on his heart. "Is my knowledge a compliment," he says sarcastically.

"It's as good as you're going to get when I'm so angry!"

He tips her chin up again, and she nearly relaxes at his touch. "I'm sorry, but you cannot fault me for wanting to protect you."

Her gaze peers into his own, wandering, searching. "Is that a compliment, too?"

He grins, and something - *something* - spreads from his chest to his toes and fingers. A warmth. A stir. A promise of something more to come.

And Dao isn't wary of it.

Kristal had been the first to climb the stairs to Nefari's parent's chamber. A few seconds behind her, Nefari follows Vale, crown gripped in hand as their feet soundlessly tread against the gods forsaken dark, steep, and slippery steps.

Nefari, ignoring the fact that they're leaving the gold behind - gold that could buy armies - says, "When or if I become queen, we should think about -"

Vale sucks in a breath. Nefari looks up, and her heart skips a beat. "What is it?" she asks softly. "Vale, what is it?"

He does not answer.

She moves to stand beside him, and she pushes both of them into the room by doing so, free hand itching to grab her dagger, which Vale still holds.

The torch lay against the stone floor, small flames reaching for the ceiling, and there, just beyond it stands Kristal and someone else. Kristal has the small, slender, and filthy woman's back pressed to her front, the edge of the sparkling inferaze sword at the woman's neck.

"Why are you here?" Kristal demands in the woman's ear. "Who are you?"

"My sweet Divine," Nefari hisses, moving past Vale, who's still frozen in his spot. She'd recognize the face of Cyllian's sister, and her mother's old handmaiden, anywhere, despite the effects of age.

"Kristal, stop! Stop! That's Beau Timida!"

Flicking her gaze to Nefari, Kristal asks, "Who?"

"Beau! Now, let her go!" Nefari sets the crown down on the nightstand by the large bed, crosses the distance,

143

and swats the sword away from Beau's neck with her cloth-wrapped hand. Beau sags from Kristal's arms, and Nefari catches her before she falls to the edge of the fireplace rug.

"How are you alive?" she demands in a whisper.

"I could ask the same of you," Beau counters, her voice raspy. She rights herself on steady feet, though she sways a bit. *My Divine, she appears so weak, so brittle.*

Nefari pulls her tight to her chest, a great hug for a missed friend. "I escaped like some of the other shadow children."

Beau hooks her chin over Nefari's shoulder and continues, "I saw the blood in your bedroom chambers and . . . well, I assumed you had died."

"Well, I didn't. It wasn't my blood."

"You smell atrocious," Beau comments with a wary laugh.

Nefari chuckles. "As do you." She pulls away, keeping her hands on the woman's upper arms as she studies her unhealthy state. "How did you survive?"

Beau shrugs. "I hid. I made it to the tunnels before your mother's blast. And after," she swallows thickly, "I've been living on meager supplies."

"And my brothers? My father?" Vale steps up beside them. His voice is steady despite his slight tremble.

Shaking her head, Beau whispers, "I am the only one I've seen in a decade, but I had hoped that some of you survived. I see my prayers have not gone unanswered."

"Your prayers were useless," Nefari grins.

"Apparently, not that useless," Kristal interjects. She sheaths her sword and then introduces herself. Beau does not acknowledge her with more than a nervous squint.

"The true Divine are gone," Nefari corrects with a glaring look at Kristal. "And they've chosen others to take their place."

Beau nods. "I assume you have a reason for traveling with someone from Salix," she grumbles. Nefari isn't sure what gave it away. The way Kristal holds herself, all prim and proper, or her accent.

Nefari hears Vale's huff of amusement but ignores it. "She's the Hope-favored."

"Hope-favored?" Beau frowns and listens as they usher her to one of her parents' chairs and explains the past ten years. Nefari skips over the harrowing parts, fearful the woman's heart would stop.

"Beau," Nefari squats down before her, "how have you really survived? This place, it's rubble and ash."

Beau tips her head, gesturing to the back of the castle. "The castle gardens. I restored them, and some of the sheep had survived." She shrugs. "I've bred and sowed and rationed."

"Have you. . ." Nefari swallows. "Have you left the Shadow Kingdom since that day?"

"No." She shakes her head. "I've wanted to, but my fear got the better of me. I've been staying here, in your parent's room. I restored it, too."

So that's what happened, Nefari thinks to herself. It wasn't some act of the Divine that kept her mother and father's things protected. It had been remade by someone who loved them both like all devoted servants love the royals.

Beau pushes her white hair from her face. There are stress lines around her eyes, and they wrinkle as she frowns. "I just couldn't stand the thought of not being close to my lady. I hope you don't mind, Nefari."

"Not at all. Don't apologize for surviving." Nefari sure won't, and in the end, all that matters is she's alive. Besides, though it was heartbreaking to see the room as it once was, she's glad the woman had something to cling to.

"Thank you," she says, her tone small. She shrinks in on herself and wipes a stray tear from her cheek.

Nefari pats her knee then looks to Vale who hovers behind the highback chair, his jaw ticking. "What do we do?"

"We take her to the Onyx Guard as soon as we leave here." His tone is a deep rumble but hushed enough that the moment of grief still lingers. "She can't stay here. Not on her own and unprotected. It's a miracle she survived."

Kristal begins to build a fire, grabbing logs from beside the hearth and stacking them neatly inside. She retrieves the torch and sparks her kindling to life. The room immediately warms.

"Can we -" Beau pauses and looks at the back of Kristal's head. She whispers, "Can we stay for a few days? Perhaps catch up?"

"You truly want to stay here? In the rubble?"

Beau nods.

In truth, Nefari wonders if she wants to stay because she doesn't trust Kristal. The way she looks at her is telling enough. She can't blame her, but unfortunately, only time will build that trust just like Nefari had learned to trust her in Kadoka City.

She looks to Vale again, and Vale inclines his head, though she can tell his mind is still whirling. The shock of Beau surviving and his family not had taken a fresh toll.

"Then, we will stay for a few days," she says with a nurturing tone. "But we have to get back to Kadoka City before the centaurs send out a hunting party. Do you have a place we can clean up? Perhaps some food?"

Rising from the chair, Beau waves for them to follow.

CHAPTER THIRTEEN

Late that night, with their bellies full and their bodies washed, Nefari falls asleep on her parents' bed and dreams a memory.

Through her mother's cracked door, she witnesses her mother bolt upright in the bed, breathing heavily as if she had a bad dream. Seven-year-old Nefari had her own bad dream moments ago and had planned to sneak into bed with her parents, but the look on her mother's face stops her in the hallway.

Sweat glistens along her mother's forehead, and she wipes it away with the heel of her hand.

Frightened further, Nefari almost runs to Beau's room. Her mother's lady would surely provide her the comfort she needed, and just as she turns away to do so, she hears her mother murmur back and forth with her father.

The words, "Queen Sieba Arsonian –" spoken by her mother are what make Nefari's heart pound. Though she's only a princess, she can't help but overhear what the grown adults are discussing. The Queen is bad. Evil. The nightmares that plague Nefari's dreams hold wraith-like creatures hovering above her, hand outstretched while the queen grins on. Nefari has never seen the queen, but her child-mind had made her wickedly beautiful with soulless black eyes.

"Queen Sieba cannot reach us, Amala," her father growls. "She cannot break through our shadows. The Shadled Forest has always protected us and will continue to do so long after you and I are gone from this realm. Not once in history has our enemy breached our shadow's protections. You needn't worry so much about it."

"You truly think our shadows will be enough?"

"They always have been."

There's a pause, and Nefari stiffens, thinking she had alerted her parents to her whereabouts, but then her mother presses on, her voice rising with each word. "That was before. That was when Fate was still alive. That was before the Realm's War when Fate had learned Despair possessed the Demon Realm's Fee and started a war across most of the realms, Davan. That was before when he was still alive. *Before*, Davan."

"There are still two other Divine gods that Despair will have to destroy before he can truly rule this realm, Amala." Father's tone is short and clipped, and Nefari winces. Her parents always fight and mostly about her.

150

She doesn't know what to make of it, but she knows she doesn't like it.

Her mother presses, "No one has seen Hope and Choice for eight years, either. For all we know, they could have transferred their power to another as Fate had done to Nefari."

Her father laughs cruelly. "And who would they transfer their power to?" He sighs. "A pirate of Widow's Bay? A crone from The Frozen Fades? A slave from Urbana? Or perhaps a centaur of the Kadoka Mountains. Bastian, maybe? Choice loved his hooved creatures. Come now, Amala. You must see how ridiculous this sounds."

Her mother growls. "Do not talk of the centaurs in such a way."

"Yes, yes, I know. You're fond of them, too." Truth be told, so is Nefari. She finds the tall and muscled creatures fascinating and learns from Bastian every time he visits.

"They've agreed to help if Queen Sieba finds our kingdom. All I have to do is call upon them, Davan. That's more than I can say about you. At least, they believe me."

Nefari hears the ruffle of cloth and prepares to bolt to Beau's chambers.

"Where are you going?" her mother hisses.

There's another pause, and Nefari holds her breath. "The conversation is the same, Amala. First, we talk about the Divine. Then, we worry over our daughter and her magic. Next, we worry about Sieba. Then, you'll start to remind me how she's a puppet to Despair." He heaves a breath. "I won't entertain this any longer. I – I can't."

Her heart leaps in her chest when his hand closes around the door handle. She jumps into the hallway shadows and leaps to Beau's chambers.

Beau immediately wakes at the sound of Nefari's sobs. "Little girl," she whispers, shocked. She pushes back her covers and dashes to Nefari's side. "What is it?"

"Momma and Pappa are fighting."

"Oh." She gathers Nefari into her arms for a tight hug then mumbles in her ear, "Would you like to sleep in my bed tonight?"

Nefari nods against her shoulder. She's always seen Beau as a second mother. "Please."

"Good, come on. Your mother won't be pleased if she sees you exhausted in the morning. She'll think you and Vale are up to your usual antics."

Beau guides her to the bed while Nefari sniffles.

Nefari wakes slowly, remembering the dream in vivid detail. She had nearly forgotten it, and her heart wrenched at the memory of her parents.

"You fell asleep," Vale comments beside her on her parent's bed. Nefari glances at him then follows his gaze to the ceiling. She hadn't meant to fall asleep, but the days have been rough.

"Yeah."

"Was it a good dream?"

Nefari rubs at her eyes. "Not particularly."

Though the covers are underneath them, their closeness sends butterflies fluttering to Nefari's stomach. To calm the blush rising to her cheeks, she listens to the soft flames that Kristal and Beau sleep before while embracing the warmth it has to offer.

The stones on the ceiling above them hold flecks of diamonds in their hard surface, making it appear as though they're gazing at the stars. In her youth, Nefari hadn't noticed, but then again, she was busy being unruly.

"Do you remember when we used to spar with wooden swords?" Nefari asks with a grin, banishing the memory entirely. Bastian wasn't the only one who taught Nefari, nor was she the only one he taught.

"One of my fonder memories." He scratches his cheek. "You used to cheat."

153

"I never cheated," she hissed. "You were taller than me and, therefore, much slower."

He chuckles. "I was not slow."

"That is not how I remember it."

He turns on the bed and stares at the side of her face until her eyes meet his. He seems to hesitate before he asks, "What are we, Nefari?"

She frowns. "What do you mean?"

Wetting his bottom lip, he amends, "Who are *we*? Together? What does this make us? Where do we stand?"

Nefari's heart hammers against her ribs because of the way he's looking at her . . . Well, this look could melt all the ice in Kadoka City. "You mean, are we still intended for one another?" He nods, and she blows out a breath. "I don't know, Vale. I don't know you anymore. I don't know *anything* anymore." She waves at his body. "You're still the same, but you're . . ."

"We're different," he finishes. He reaches and tucks a lock of hair behind her ear.

"Exactly."

"You're beautiful without the shadows shrouding your face," he murmurs. Where his fingers graze her skin, heat rises. "I expect nothing of you, nor of *this*, but I do feel things for you. These are feelings that have never gone away. Not in ten years, and not before then."

She lets the pause settle between them. "If I am to be queen, if I am to cleave the darkness like everyone is asking of me, I don't know how many distractions I can handle."

"I know."

"If I am to free my people, I need unbiased people by my side."

"I know."

"If we become romantically involved, that breaks those two rules."

He smiles then grips her chin. "I know."

She turns to face him fully. "Is that all you have to say?"

"Yes," he answers simply. Nefari braces herself as he leans and feathers his lips against hers. His lips are soft and kind and gentle, and an unfamiliar tingling sensation blooms in her stomach.

He pulls away, too quickly. "But I won't give up."

"You wouldn't be you if you did," she croaks out. She clears her throat, an unflattering sound, but she's never been spectacular at romance. "Just like I will make sure you're safe from all this."

She stretches and grabs the crown from her mother's nightstand. "Give me your dagger." Her own are lying near Beau, placed there so the woman will feel safer around Kristal. She didn't ask for them - Nefari gave them willingly, knowing the skeptical thought racing through Beau's mind.

"Why?"

She holds out her hand and raises her eyebrows in wordless demand. He pulls it from the sheath at his hip and hands it to her. She takes it and pries one of the stones out with little effort. "Here. Take this."

"What is this? What are you doing?"

She settles it in his waiting palm and sets the crown back down. "It'll protect you as my ring has done for me."

"You're sure?"

She nods. "I wouldn't break apart my family heirloom if I wasn't."

He considers the stone between pinched fingers then pockets it. "How many days are we staying?"

"Just a few to let Beau get comfortable with Kristal."

He huffs. "No one could get comfortable with Salix blood around."

Mockingly shoving his shoulder, she grins at him. "You need to get over it, too. And as for your question . . . Let me think on where we stand, okay?"

The side of his lips quirk. He takes her hand in his, and his warmth seeps into her fingers. "That's all I ask."

CHAPTER FOURTEEN

Inside the carriage that's traveling through Loess's main capital, Ortaloo, Patrix Eiling drums his fingers on his thighs. He would much rather be on a horse's back or, hell, walking than be paraded through the streets like someone with royal blood.

He does have royal blood . . . *but that's not the point,* he tells himself.

Under the hot afternoon sun and embraced by the docks humidity, they left the ship quickly and found the carriage waiting for them. Being paraded around in such an extravagant carriage with the best horses Sutherland has to offer is an invitation to be gawked at by the peasants and knights and noblemen.

Patrix almost didn't enter it, but Emory nearly dragged him inside. The carriage interior of plush cushions and fine fabrics offer little in the way of comfort. Not with the heat.

The patrons of many classes wander through the numerous pop-up shops throughout the fish market, spreading their money sparingly or richly. It's all frivolous to Patrix, a view that makes him sick. He'd much prefer the view of the brothels at the east end of Ortaloo, but he isn't so lucky to be taken through those parts of the city.

Some of the patrons attempt to peer inside upon passing. Patrix scoots back until his spine hits the wall of the carriage, tucked neatly into its shadows. "I'd rather be anywhere but here." He is no royal. He abandoned any and all titles when he was barely an adult.

"Who would have thought the great Patrix Eiling would be hiding like a girl with a crush," Emory grumbles.

Ten years ago, having packed his bags with his belongings, he had set out on his own with barely a goodbye to his father and protesting mother who begged at the threshold of their home. He couldn't get away from his parents and his reputation as a wild child fast enough.

First, he hitched a ride and traveled to Sutherland's capital, Hartford, to see what the forest-laden city had to offer. Though he did fall in love with a saddle maker's daughter and had his heart broken by her in a matter of weeks, the benign horse breeding folk offered less than Urbana's lucrative Black Market that called to him on a deep rebellious level.

Heart fully broken, his adventures indeed took him to the Black Market, and it was there that he remade himself.

Despite his secretly royal blood, it didn't stop him from quickly making friends with their royals, however. In fact, the Black Market was where he met them. And with a little wine at one particularly dark tavern, they entrusted their secrets upon him.

Ironic, indeed. But no royal knew who he truly was, and he preferred it that way. Here, everyone would whisper about the Queen's nephew's return, and soon, it'll reach from one villager to the last before he even walks through the castle gates.

He can still smell the sea on himself, a clinging reminder of where he was born. The scent doesn't settle well with him. It makes memories crash back like the waves against the shore.

To Emory's dismay, Patrix moves the curtains of the carriage so there's only a small window to peep out of. He is not something to be gawked at.

"I don't want to be here," he mumbles again. "Turn this carriage around."

Emory straightens himself. "No."

Patrix curses under his breath.

Coming to Loess was one thing; arriving only to hear word that his father knows he's here and had sent a carriage is another. He had wanted to avoid his father entirely. Now, he has no choice. At least his mother will smooth things between them, providing that buffer between strict father and wild son.

"Will you sit still," Emory grumbles. The carriage jostles in a hole within the dirt road, and Emory grasps the wooden rail above his head.

"I can't."

"Well, at least, pretend. You're making me nervous."

Patrix quirks a brow. "You should be nervous. You're going to beseech a Queen to help the Rebel Legion and ask for her daughter's hand in marriage. Though the Queen is giving, that's a tall order for anyone to accept."

"Well, when you put it that way." He doesn't say anything more because, as the market comes to an end, destruction follows.

Village homes, some still smoking, are completely destroyed.

Sharing a look, Emory and Patrix whip the curtains back right when the smoke tickles their noses. "What happened here?"

The coachman turns to answer through the wide-open window at his back. "An army tried to invade. It lasted three long days."

"Invade?" Patrix asks, incredulous. No one invades gentle Loess. "Which army?"

"The Queen of Salix's."

"Why?" Emory inquires.

"Isn't it obvious?" the coachman snipes. "She's no longer satisfied with Loess's desire to be neutral in her war. She wants our ships and our army."

"Over my aunt's dead body," Patrix murmurs to himself.

"Were there . . ." Emory swallows. "Were any harvested?"

The coachman turns back around and takes a long pause. Over his shoulder, he answers, "A few. No royals, though. They came on pirate ships straight from Okaton." Okaton was directly across from Loess, a few days' travel across Widows Bay, and home to all pirates. Their markets make the Black Market child's play. There are rumors that their slaves do not survive a month's worth of servitude.

Emory looks back to Patrix as they pull up to the castle. The sturdy walls are left completely untouched. Not even a scorch mark. Loess's army and villagers had done a wondrous job protecting the castle and the royals within.

White bricks gleam brightly in the sun, and its golden arches blind Patrix's eyes. He's never been fond of the elaborate castle with pillars and gems and pristine gargoyles, but he couldn't deny that the fishing industry was lush enough to pay for it and its upkeep.

Two guards are posted outside the wrought iron doors, and beside them, the princess of Loess and Patrix's father.

The princess, Alissia, has gleaming bright gold hair, a contrast to Patrix's father, who looks exactly like Patrix, albeit quite older than he remembered. The stress of his job - the Queen's informant and trusted right hand - had been rough on his appearance.

"There she is," Emory whispers, wistful in nature.

The princess's ruby-red-jeweled crown is small atop her head, and her cheeks are bright when she smiles broadly at their carriage.

"There be your maiden," Patrix grumbles.

"And there, your father." Emory squints. "He looks angry."

"He's always angry when it comes to me."

"Well, you haven't been home in what, a decade? Longer?"

"A decade, though it feels shorter."

The carriage pulls to a halt, and the coachman hops down from his high perch. Their carriage door opens, letting in the briny air, and Emory climbs out while the coachman fetches their meager belongings. The coachman carries the worn saddlebags to an awaiting servant just inside the castle, returning to his horses once the servant disappears inside.

Grumbling under his breath, Patrix steps out, too. He ignores the embrace Emory and princess Alissia share. He doesn't greet his cousin, who's busy with her affections as he makes his way around the carriage, patting the horse on the nose as he does so. The horse pins his ears back and attempts to bite him.

A few feet away from the horse, he stops and stuffs his hands into his pockets. The hot sun beats against his back, but the sweat perspiring there is refreshed by the warm breeze.

"He can meet me halfway," he says softly to himself. "Come on, dadd-o. Come greet your troublesome son."

With a huff and snarl, his father crosses the distance on the white-stoned, paved path. "I see you haven't changed."

He quirks a brow. "I see you haven't, either." He has half a mind to return to the surly horse. The horse would be better company.

"That is no way to talk to your father."

"Produce my mother, and see my attitude change." Patrix has always liked his soft-hearted mother. She was kind to him, overlooked his quirks and faults. She was the buffer and the glue.

"You'll have to go to the east graveyard for that, I'm afraid. The one by the armory."

"Graveyard?" Patrix stiffens. "She's dead?"

His father softens fractionally and nods. "This time last year."

"And you're so bent up about it, I see," he hisses.

His father sighs as Emory and the princess move inside the castle. "I mourned her loss, Trixie. She was mourned and buried with honor."

Though Patrix's mother was soft-hearted, she never loved her husband. She loved another man, and though their marriage carried on, her devotion was never to the man she vowed herself to. Patrix knew all of this, even at a young age, and often wondered if his true father was the one before him or this other man he had never met.

It matters not.

"You could have sent word," he ground out.

"To where? To the pockets of darkness you squat in? Or through the terrible company you keep? Perhaps the whores of Urbana? I'm sure they'd love to pass you a raven."

Heat rises to Patrix's face. "The Rebel Legion," he grinds out. "You could have sent a raven to the Legion. They would have gotten the message to me."

He shakes his head. "Would it have made a difference?"

Patrix's hands ball into fists, and he has the desire to growl at his father.

"Why are you here, Trixie? Surely, it can't be for a reunion. You made that clear when you left; you wanted nothing to do with Loess and your courtly duties as nephew to the Queen."

Patrix shoves the thought of his dead mother down deep inside him. He refuses to let his father get the best of him. "I escorted Emory. I won't be staying long."

"And what does dear Emory have for business with the queen? It appears as though he came for your cousin, and not for the audience."

"Oh, he came for the audience, but his father believes he came for her."

"His father is the Urbana General, yes?"

"That's the one."

As if the couple is being called, the princess's giggle spills out the nearest castle window as the two make their way to the inner courtyard.

"Come, talk with me as we join the young couple and make sure they don't find themselves in precarious positions before they wed. Your aunt would never forgive me."

Patrix follows his father, observing the subtle, swirling designs in the arches as they pass underneath them, then bowing their greeting to both guards before they enter the castle.

Respect is always shone here, but truths are hardly ever told. The kingdom may be serene, but it doesn't stop the usual courtly gossip. However, like all kingdoms, gossip is welcome. Gossip is the platform that builds one's reputation, and Patrix's reputation couldn't get any worse than it already is. He'll deserve no respect for deserting his country, and he's unlucky enough to not have been tossed out already. He'd be okay with that.

The cooler and dim hallways enfold them, and they stride with little purpose, passing pictures and windows and servant bedrooms. Servants pass them, giggling as they catch eyes with Patrix, and he grins wickedly at them. Their giggles increase, and his father snorts.

To the left of the hallway, the castle opens to the sky, letting the sun shine on the inner courtyard garden through its entrance just ahead. Roses grow here, and the branches of small trees reach in every direction. A gardener waters the flowers, paying no mind to those roaming the hall, nor Emory and Alissia, who take their seat on a bench among white-petaled vines.

"You should tell me what Emory wants with the queen. Perhaps I can help the young lad."

Patrix looks at the side of his father's face and then stops, returning his hands to his pockets. His father stops, too, and whirls to face him questioningly. "Trixie?"

"Don't call me that," Patrix grinds out. "I'm not the same boy who left here. My name is of many, but Trixie is not one of them."

"My boy." His father strides to him and cups his cheeks with his hot hands. "No matter how we get along, you will always be Trixie in my heart."

If you have a heart, Patrix thinks. He rips his face from his father's hands. "The Rebel Legion."

"What of it?"

"There was a Harvest Storm, and now . . ." Patrix sighs out his frustration. What he's about to divulge cannot be taken back, but sooner or later, the news will get out. It's best to hear it from him. "The princess of the Shadow Kingdom is alive."

Blinking, his father takes a moment to adjust to both pieces of news. "She's alive? And in the Rebel Legion, I presume."

"Sort of. My point is that your kingdom isn't the only one that has been invaded, and *your* queen isn't the only one who has been challenged."

"*Our* queen. She will always be *our* queen, no matter how far you travel." His father strokes his beard. "And I'm to presume Emory wants to bring this to the queen's attention."

"Yes."

"To get her to join the war."

"Yes."

"That'll never happen," he declares quickly.

Patrix crosses his arms. "Then, you'll continue to endure Queen Seiba's wrath."

"You mean Despair's?"

This time, Patrix blinks. "You know about Despair's possession of the Salix queen?"

"Bah," his father spits. "Everyone does by now. She's not hiding it anymore. Don't you forget you're not the only spy in the realm."

The thought chills Patrix even though he already knew this. "And yet, you sit on your hands."

He shakes his head. "It is not up to me, boy. It is up to the queen."

Patrix shrugs. "Then, change her mind."

"You know how stubborn she can be, but I will back young Emory's beseeching if this is what you are asking of me."

"It is."

"Then, consider it done. Will you be there, too?"

Patrix wrinkles his nose. "Unfortunately." Because he has to see the job done for Bastian's and Nefari's sake, even though both probably want to skewer him by now.

CHAPTER FIFTEEN

Sibyl Withervein hisses when Swen tries to pass her a mug of tea. His particular brew has never pleased her. She remembers the first time she tried it and how she spat it back out as soon as the sweet taste coated her tongue. She prefers bitter things.

Swen shrugs and places the mug by her elbow at his desk anyway. Then, they both return to watching Bastian pace.

"Are you sure she's fine?"

"I already told you, she is in the Shadow Kingdom. She is fine. They both are fine." Sibyl doesn't tell him that by saying both, she means Vale and Nefari. She hasn't told him that Vale is alive, for that is Fari's story to tell when she returns. She'll let him think what he wants.

He whirls to face her, eyes wild. "She should be on her way back by now. What is she doing there?"

"Growing," Sibyl explains with a grin. "Laying her past to rest. Let her be, Bastian. She will return when she's ready."

"But, she has the crown?"

"She already said so," Swen interjects. "Young Sibyl is right. You fret for naught. Perhaps it is time you go home and get a proper night's rest."

Sibyl stands from her chair, borrowed from Dao's desk, and crosses the cluttered room. She stops Bastian's pacing with a hand on his arm. "She will return. I have seen your reunion, and I have seen new friends. For now, just be happy about that. All will be well."

With a grind of his jaw, he curtly nods.

After a brief and unpleasant conversation with his father about returning home to fulfill his obligations instead of "traipsing around the entire realm and trading secrets," Patrix steps outside the castle. It's like a breath of fresh air, though he nearly chokes on it due to the humidity. In this moment, he misses the cold and unforgiving air of the Kadoka Mountains.

This time, he ignores the bowing guards and the beat of the sun on his cheeks. His hooves rest against the scalding stone path, and he inhales deeply a few more times before he takes in his surroundings. The castle has always felt too small for him even though it is anything but.

Patrix turns and looks at the broken houses then further down where the market begins. He jolts in surprise at what he finds.

Down the way, shopping at the nearest tent with many bright-colored fish on display is Yayla, the attractive and elusive woman from the ship. She chats with the merchant then grins at whatever the merchant says. Patrix smiles, and with an extra skip in his step, he crosses the castle entrance and travels down the path.

"Do you live nearby?" he asks over her shoulder.

She spooks, jumping from her skin, and whirls to face him. The dead fish in her hand flops and nearly drops. "By the gods, do not sneak up on me like that."

"Is there something to be afraid of?" He places a hand on his heart. "Am I frightening?"

"You're something alright," she grumbles, turning back to the merchant and digging a few coins from her jingling purse. She hands the gold pieces to the merchant, and the merchant bows deeply. "And to answer your original question, where I live is none of your business. If it were, I'd ask you if you lived in the castle and why."

"So, you were watching me." Patrix feels flattered.

"You're hard to overlook." She travels to the next tent and peers at the red fruits on display. "And no, that wasn't meant as a compliment, so you can depuff your chest."

Patrix laughs. "Will you eat with me?"

Yayla holds up her fish and gestures to it. "The fish and I have plans."

"Tomorrow, then?"

She peers at him sidelong then moves out of the way of roaming patrons. "Are you trying to court me or bed me?"

"Does it make a difference?"

"I'm interested in neither." She picks up a piece of fruit and sniffs it.

She stiffens as he leans and whispers in her ear. "I'm trying to feed you. Let me feed you."

She smirks. "Will there be breast milk of another tame beasty or just your usual wine and ale?"

"Whatever you'd like."

She turns her smirk on him. "Did wolves raise you? Most satyrs won't touch milk, and I swear by my parents' life they live off ale. I know where you fall, so why are you trying to be otherwise?"

He crosses his arms, "I'm not most satyrs. I'll bend to a lady's will."

"Will you now?" She cocks her head to the side. "For little ol' me?"

"You may be little, but -" She shucks him on the arm with her elbow. "Tomorrow? Noon?"

She wrinkles her delicate nose. "Two days from now. I'll bring the breast milk."

He laughs as she walks away, hips swaying.

The night of his date, Patrix fidgets in his outfit inside the Loess throne room. The blue tunic, trousers, and cape are fit for kings and itch terribly around the arms. To his displeasure, his father made him wear it. "You will not see the queen looking like a rat," he had said.

After he bathed and dressed, a male servant was sent in to trim his beard and comb his hair, tying it neatly at the nape when he was finished. When he was presentable, he then led Patrix to his beckoned destination.

Beckoned. He was beckoned! Patrix was not some courtly-nonsense-or-other to be called upon. He would arrive when he felt ready!

He grumbles under his breath and takes in his surroundings. He shouldn't be here. He should be preparing to meet Yayla, and if this ran long, he'd miss it entirely. He has one chance with her. One. He isn't going to mess this up.

Made of fish bones and fishing nets that wind around aged wood, the glorious throne sits on the gold dais. The throne is too large for a queen, but Patrix has always liked the idea of his aunt ruling. She's fair and just but swift to slam her fist against the throne's arm when news displeases her.

He didn't fear the queen, however. Not like the others waiting nervously in the hall for their audience. When she was still a princess, she had been kind to him. They often played together in the courtyard, plucking the roses and dashing to her room with them to wish upon petals.

Her daughter sits on a fairly normal, high-backed chair next to her, while Emory, in just as fine clothes as Patrix, bends his knee in respect onto the white stone floor before them. The cloth wrapped around his head slips, and he adjusts it quickly.

He continues his survey. The entire room reminds Patrix of the sun that beats down on Loess. The high polished wood beams almost glow due to the floor-to-ceiling windows behind the dais. White marble pillars hold up the high ceiling, painted with gold and crimson murals from top to bottom. Some say those murals were painted with the blood of past kings and queens, but as

Patrix grew older, he knew them to be lies - fables told to make citizens who beseech the royals to think twice while in the presence of the blood of Loess's history. Patrix never shared this notion. He knew the realm was big, and he wanted to see what it had to offer him, even at a young age.

"Why would I ever agree to give you my army when I turned down the Queen of Salix so blatantly?" Queen Lorilie Eiling asks. Her brown hair matches that of her brother's and, in turn, Patrix's own. She raises an eyebrow at Emory when he rises back to his feet. "Famed as they are for saving the villages close to their territory, what's to say the Rebel Legion won't retaliate when I decline as Queen Seiba had?"

Emory shakes his head. "They're not like that."

So far, the boy has held his own in the queen's presence, but when his father, who stands behind the queen, whispers in the queen's ear, Patrix fidgets uncertainly. His father has gone back on his word before, and he wouldn't be surprised if he does so today.

Lorilie does not take her eyes off Emory. "You come here, asking for my daughter's hand in marriage and then for my army at no cost. You gain allies within my court before you utter a word to me, and now you stand on my audience floor as righteous and confident as ever." She perches forward on her throne. "Why would you think I'd agree to any of it, Emory Vinborne,

177

General's son of Urbana. A union between the two would be anything but destructive."

Emory's confidence deflates. "No, my Queen. I -"

"I am not your queen. The last time we trusted another kingdom, my father and mother were destroyed in the Shadow Kingdom's Harvest Storm."

"My queen-" He clears his throat, and Patrix cringes. The boy was doing so well. "Your grace." He bows, quick and brief. "I -"

Patrix steps forward. "This sort of union would strengthen your hold on not only your kingdom, but you'd have better intelligence on the war and what may knock on the castle door, so to speak."

The queen squints. "I like you, Patrix. I always have, but if you side with them, so help me -"

"Hear him out, Mother," the princess whispers, but the queen does not spare her daughter a glance.

When the silence stretches, Patrix moves to Emory's side. "I understand that joining the Rebel Legion - joining the Princess of the Shadow People - at no coin or compensation, is a tall order, but it is no longer something you can ignore."

"I can ignore what I please."

"Indeed, but you need protection, now more than ever. *They* need protection. And by joining the Rebel Legion,

Nefari Ashcroft, and agreeing to this marriage, you would be ensuring your future - Loess's future. Urbana wouldn't dream of storming your castle after such a union. And perhaps, in the end, it'll strengthen their resolve to break away from Salix's hold."

"That's preposterous," the queen spits, but she chews on the inside of her cheek when she slumps in her throne, considering her options just the same.

His father softly explains, "If you do nothing, eventually the kingdom will perish under the weight of Salix. What happened in our own city, just the other day, can not be ignored. It is a warning for what's to come, and we need allies."

"Urbana will never align with us," Lorilie answers. "No matter contracts and marriages."

"But who says their General won't protect his only son and his son's bride?" Patrix counters.

The queen's eyes narrow once more, and the pause smothers the room, smothers Patrix.

Eventually, the queen flourishes her hand. "Go. I will think on both proposals, but for now . . ." She snaps her fingers at the servants waiting, unseen, for her beck and call against the far wall. "Enjoy what I have to offer for your return, Patrix. As for Emory and my daughter," she looks to her daughter, "You will be supervised at every hour when together. You are not married yet, and you will treat your relationship as such. Am I understood?"

The group collectively nods, and Emory and Patrix turn on their heels and march from the throne room. Once in the hall and past the other citizens nervously waiting, Emory sags with relief.

Patrix pats him on the shoulder. "You did well, boy. You did well."

"And now?"

He blows out a breath. "Now, we wait and pray to the gods that my father can do the rest."

"I thought you didn't trust him."

"Right now, I have no choice."

Patrix pats him one more time then leaves to meet Yayla in his appointed chambers. The servants had been instructed to have a meal prepared and waiting for his and her arrival. He prayed they had been successful, for he aims to impress.

CHAPTER SIXTEEN

Patrix stretches awake as Yayla's hand caresses the hair on his chest. The feeling is pleasant, and not many have done it before her, whether they were paid for or he had been simply lucky one night.

Last night, he had been lucky. Though they had barely spoken during their meal the previous night, it hadn't taken long for them to find their way to his bed.

The morning sun splashes across his chambers, and outside, seagulls and chickens squawk their greetings. His windows are wide open, left that way to allow cool night air to caress their naked skin.

He blinks, eyes on the ceiling, as he listens to the sounds of the waking market, soft murmurs that spread up the castle wall and to his second-story room.

In the distance, bells ring on fishing boats sailing to capture their daily bounty.

Yayla stirs beside him.

He lifts his head and peers at her. "Good morning."

She blinks sleepily while her knife on the nightstand glints almost warningly behind her. When he discovered she had one hidden on her person, he was smitten. A woman who can take care of herself is an attractive quality to Patrix.

His grin broadens, having immediately remembered the night before in perfect detail.

"Morning," she answers.

"Sleep well?"

"Hmm," she purrs and scoots closer, her leg hooking over his. Her hair is a tangled mess around her horns, a charming look in his opinion.

He touches her cheek and brings his lips to hers for a quick peck. Their softness sends a tingle to his hooves. "Remember how you said you wouldn't sleep with me?"

She smirks and slaps him on the chest. "I do not like to visit my bad decisions. And you snore."

"I do not," he professes in mock offense.

She flips back the sheets, removes herself from him, and climbs off the bed. Propped on his elbows, he watches her bend and grab her clothes from the floor.

"Leaving so soon? I thought we could . . ." his voice trails off while his eyebrows wiggle suggestively.

"Not a chance," she says smugly while she ties her trousers. "This was a one-time deal."

"And what about breakfast?" he demands. "A lady needs to eat."

"A lady can grab a meal at the market on her way out of here."

He frowns. "You still won't tell me what you're doing in Loess?" Last night, during their meager conversation, he had discovered that she truly does not live here. Like Patrix, she roams, and she hadn't planned to stay here for more than a few days.

She grabs her knife from the nightstand and tucks it into its small, secret sheath inside her trousers. "I told you. I'm here for a job and nothing more." She gestures her hand, pointing a finger back and forward between them. "This was a one-time thing. It'll be good for you if I never see you again."

His frown deepens as his heart stings. "Is that so? You'll dismiss me so soon?"

Shaking the wrinkles from her tunic, she peers at him sidelong. "As I said, it'll be good for you."

The bedroom door bursts open as she pulls her tunic over her head. Patrix grabs the sheets and scrambles to cover himself. His father steps through the door, glowering at what he sees before him, imagining what, exactly, had transpired here.

"At it again, I see," he insists to Patrix.

Patrix wraps the sheet around his waist, heaves his legs over the side of the bed, and stands. "As I'll ever be."

"Shall I leave?" Yayla asks with a quirk of her delicate brow.

"Yes," his father answers at the same time Patrix says, "No."

Yayla chuckles, unaffected by the tense mood swapped between father and son. "I'll go. Patrix, it was an interesting date. Memorable." She places a hand on her chest and mockingly adds, "I'll keep it with me until the end of time." She crosses the room, grabs a green apple from the table's centerpiece, and bites into it as she exits the room. The door shuts softly behind her.

Patrix drops the sheets. "I think I'm in love, Father."

"You are not. Why can't you act courtly?"

Searching the floor, Patrix hunts for his trousers. He scowls then finds them dangling from his father's finger. He crosses the room and snatches them, shaking the wrinkles free and sliding his legs inside. "What do you want?"

His father folds his arms across his pressed tunic. "The queen has made her final decision."

Bare-chested, Patrix pulls his shoulders back and prepares for the worst news. It could go either way, but if he has to go back to the Legion with bad news . . . Well, he doesn't want to endure Bastian's rage and Fari's further disappointment.

"She agreed to let Emory and the princess Alissia marry." He holds up a finger to stop Patrix from saying anything. "And, she agreed to aid you in your mission for the Rebel Legion. She's already gathered the troops out by the docks, who await your instruction, and she has sent a raven to Sutherland to do the same. Their warhorses could change the face of this mess."

He sucks in a breath. Sutherland and Loess are neighboring countries, often trading fish goods with their finely bred horses. To have an army on horses and on sea . . . Patrix can barely wrap his head around it. "She'll - They'll help Nefari?"

"If Sutherland agrees, yes. As for the queen, she loves her nephew. Do not take her love for granted." His father inclines his head then stuffs his hands into his trouser pockets. "Are you going to thank her, or are you going to leave?"

Patrix shrugs. "Leave. There's nothing left for me to do." He didn't add that he has every intention of convincing Yayla to go with him.

"You could stay and be my son," his father suggests in a begrudging manner. "You could take your place beside me."

"Oh?" Patrix sucks on a tooth, refusing to consider both options. "I am grateful for what you've done on mine and the Legion's behalf, but I stopped being your son ten years ago. My place is with the Legion. My allegiance is with the Queen of the Shadow Kingdom." *If she'll have me,* he adds to himself. But that's a problem for another day.

His father opens his mouth to retort, but shouts and screams begin in the streets. Scowling, Patrix strides across his room and pokes his head out the window, feeling his father close behind.

Down the way, by the water, foreign ships sail to their shores, releasing flaming cannons on fishing boats as they pass.

"The Salix army," his father breathes. "They've returned!"

"Not the Salix army," Patrix corrects quietly. "Those are pirates." The black sails that whip in the breeze are unmistakable. He recognizes one who waits in the bay as the Wench, the most deadly pirate ship across Widow's Bay and captained by the Pirate Queen herself.

Patrix swallows thickly then glances directly below his window. A small pirate raiding group battles with the guards of the castle. Patrix's heart thunders in his ears. And as soon as the men are cut down with swords that gleam bloody-red in the hot morning sun, they dip inside the gates.

"My Divine," his father whispers.

Patrix barks, "Get the princess and Emory to safety!" He heads to retrieve his sword from where it rests by his chamber's door. "Bring them here, bolt the door, and don't let anyone inside! Not even me."

"What are you going to do?" his father asks, quickly following him out into the brightening hall.

"I'll get the queen." At this hour, she'll be in her chambers, readying herself for the day. "Go!" he waves his sword as he strides down the hall. "Go!"

His father stops him with a hand on his shoulder. Patrix whirls to face him, witnessing his father's wild eyes. "Be careful," is all he pleads. He turns and jogs to the princess's chambers at the far end of the castle, each footstep punctuated with the screams spreading up from the first floor.

Patrix watches him go then turns on his hooves and darts in the other direction. More shouts are heard throughout the castle, and it propels him to move quicker, faster, hooves clanking loudly about. Torches light his way, and as he bends the corner to the last door, his hoof kicks a half-eaten apple. "What in the -"

The apple bounces into the adjacent wall then spirals as it heads farther away from him. He watches it go until it stops at someone's feet.

Yayla.

She stands outside the queen's chambers, staring within. The doors are wide open, and he skids to a halt beside her.

"What are you doing? Run! Flee back to my chambers and wait there with the princess!"

She turns wide eyes upon him, and it's then that he sees the knife dripping blood onto her hand.

"Wh - what are you doing?" he softly asks of her, the breath leaving his lungs. He backs away a step.

"I'm sorry, Patrix. I didn't want it to happen, but I had no choice. I-I- I'm sorry." She looks into the chambers one last time and brings a bloody hand to her chin.

Wetting his bottom lip, Patrix steps inside the chambers, and there, sprawled on the floor, is the Queen of Loess. His ears ring at the sight, and he moves an inch closer, the tips of his hooves touching the queen's puddle of blood.

She did this. Sweet and sassy Yayla- "You did this." He whips around to face her, demanding answers, but a fist connects with his temple, and blackness descends.

Vale leads Nefari out of the castle and to the back where Beau's crops sparingly grow. Some of the crops, encased by broken fences, are leaning with the weight of their bounty. They pass the crops and head to the stable beyond where horses used to whinny and stalls would wait to be mucked by any unfortunate person who broke the rules. Nefari and Vale had been two of those individuals, often caught in their antics within the castle. It is a chore that, as an adult, Nefari still doesn't enjoy. The thought reminds her of Astra, stabled back in Calhoun, waiting for their return.

"Where are we going?"

"Here," he says, stopping in his tracks and turning in a circle. "There are plenty of shadows. Bend them."

"I can't just bend them, Vale."

"Try," he insists impatiently. "Close your eyes, and try."

Begrudgingly, Nefari does as she's been asked, but nothing happens. The shadows stay where they are. "It's not working," she declares angrily.

He holds out his arms and encompasses the kingdom. "Here, you can practice your magic, and no wraiths nor no queens, will know what you do."

"Well, isn't that a way to my heart," she mocks. If this is a romantic gesture, he needs to work on it.

He looks at her hands. "Pull out your starlight sword." Within a second, she does, and he grabs her wrist to examine it, twisting it this way and that. "Does it hurt?"

"To hold it?" He flicks his gaze to hers, as good as any nod. "No."

He gently releases her wrist. "You need to learn to use both magics together. All your skills need to be honed as one if you are to truly cleave the darkness, Nefari."

"I can't." She looks at her feet. "I don't know how."

"You don't know how?" He chuffs. "Or you're too frightened to?"

Nefari peers back into his eyes and juts her chin. "I am not afraid," she lies.

The side of his lips turns upward. "Everyone is afraid of something. And when we conquer one fear, we find another." He invades her space. "You cannot cleave the darkness until you can fully command some part of the light, until you explore its absolute depths, but that won't be enough. Despair is pure darkness. You are pure light. Afraid or not, you need to be ready."

"And if I'm not good enough?" His nearness makes her head spin, and her words came out as nothing but a breath.

He brushes his thumb against her cheek then leans in to press his lips to hers. This kiss is feather-light, but

Nefari's toes curl just the same. Against them, he murmurs, "Then, we all die."

"And Amoon? Do you think I can eventually save her? Do you think -" Nefari swallows as tears spring to her eyes. "Do you think she's still alive?"

He leans away with a frown. "I believe there is hope. My Divine, Nefari. The Hope-favored is your friend. If you don't have hope, then you have nothing. Okay? Have hope."

She nods against his hand then straightens her shoulders and tucks her tears away. "Who am I sparring with?"

He moves away from her, backing several feet. "Not me."

She quirks a brow. "Is Vale Riversdale afraid of my starlight?"

"A fool wouldn't fear it." He points at her. "You're sparring with yourself."

CHAPTER SEVENTEEN

"Are you ready?" Vale asks, shouldering the pack with the crown inside.

Vale, Nefari, Kristal, and Beau wait by the creep, the deep swirling shadow that will take them from the Shadow Kingdom and back to the dark depths of the Shadled. Nefari is the only one in shadow form, opting to be the one who will transport them. They're to journey to the Kadoka Mountains, and though Nefari didn't want to come here, now she doesn't want to leave.

Aside from the magic lesson, their two days spent here have been quiet, peaceful. At any moment, she felt as though she could turn a corner and find her parents lurking about, and sometimes - *sometimes* - she got the whiff of her mother's scent.

During their few days' stay, they never dipped into the throne room. Beau had said it was nothing but ash, not even a skull to mourn. Nefari didn't want to see it. She didn't want anything tainting her resolve to claim who she was: the Shadow Queen. Seeing that . . . *destruction* would make her fear another thing. Seeing that destruction would make her fear her own magic, Fate-blessed or not. She wouldn't do that to herself, and truth be told, Vale wouldn't let her do that to herself either, though he was just as frightened at the idea of laying witness to it. His father, traitorous mother, and brother died in Nefari's mother's blast of magic. He wouldn't know which pile of ash was who.

So, instead of venturing far, Vale, Kristal, and Beau had helped her restore her drafty chambers. They had righted the bed, fixed the dresser, and restacked the brittle logs waiting by the fireplace. It was all done through tears and sweat, but somehow, it had helped her reassemble herself, to build her resolve to see her true duties through. They couldn't, however, scrub Amoon's blood from the floor.

But she will be queen. She will see her people freed. She will cleave the darkness if for anything but to return here with her people and make it whole again.

"Yes. Yes, I'm ready," she whispers to him, a wordless vow to return. She turns to Beau. "Are you?"

"No, but I need to." In the few days they've been here, the color had finally returned to her cheeks, rosy splotches in her human form.

"Then, we will do it together," she reassures her.

Kristal nods, having grown a liking for Amala's past lady. "Together." They all grasp hands.

"Wait, wait, wait," Beau pleads. "I should grab my -"

"Beau," Nefari whispers, tugging her hand to gain her attention. Her tone is calm and reassuring as she speaks to the aging lady. "It'll be here when we come home."

Kristal squeezes Beau's hand. "Whatever you wanted to grab is not going anywhere. It's safe here."

Beau looks back to Nefari. "Home?"

Nefari grins and lights the black shadow crown atop her head. "Home."

"I like the sound of that," Vale says with a small grin.

"Okay," Beau speaks meekly. "Okay."

Releasing a deep sigh, Nefari pulls the group forward, and they walk into the swirls of shadows, hoping like hell that they will, indeed, return. Because they will. They have to. She'll see it so even if something happens and she's not to return with them.

The creep's shadows yank against their clothes and skin, but Nefari keeps walking, keeps tugging them along through the darkness.

As soon as they're on the other side, Beau gasps in the Shadled air. They release each other's hands as she says, "I had forgotten what it felt like, the way the darkness caresses the skin at the end." She glances around. "Where are all the Diabolus Beetles?"

There's an ominous feeling in the air, and Nefari doesn't miss it. Perhaps it's because they left the kingdom. Perhaps this realm truly is affected by the dark magic of the Queen of Salix. Perhaps she just wants nothing more than to turn back around and . . .

Hand on the hilt of her sword, Kristal begins walking. "Let's get back." She doesn't waste any time as she takes the thin trail they had followed into the Shaddled. Nefari notes that she doesn't seem to notice the feeling like she does.

Nefari squints at the darkness down the way while Vale pats Beau's shoulder as they too begin walking. "I don't know, but remember, no shadow jumping outside the kingdom. It'll alert the wraiths, and -" He pauses when a breeze brings about a stench.

Goosebumps rise over Nefari's arms.

Everyone except for Kristal stops and looks up into the trees beyond. Nefari's heart skips a beat, and for a moment, she allows light to linger at her fingertips. She had promised Bastian she wouldn't use magic, but she recognizes the smell and the wrongness, would know it anywhere despite it being a decade.

"What the bloody-Divine is it?" Kristal questions, turning to see why the group stopped. Down the way, just barely visible through the dark, a cloak whisks, pushed by the breeze.

"Don't move," Vale orders softly. "Don't move, and maybe it won't see us."

"Vale," Nefari warns, snuffing her light because she knows that *creature* isn't their only guest.

"A wraith," Beau whispers, voice trembling. "Did it - did it detect the shadow jump?"

Neither Vale nor Nefari answers her. There is no right answer. It was either the shadow jump or . . . it had been waiting for them.

"What is going on?" Kristal quietly demands through clenched teeth.

"Get your sword ready," Nefari answers in the same fashion.

"Why?"

"Because there are wraiths," Vale answers. "And crones."

Having heard their conversation, the wraith moves closer. It doesn't matter how the wraith knew to be here. It doesn't matter how it knew which shadow they'd jump through. All that matters is how they survive.

"Do you still have your stone?" Nefari asks him distractedly. He nods. "Good."

A crone's cackle follows the wraith's movement, echoing from seemingly everywhere. Then another after the first. Then another, until there's a chorus of raspy cruel laughter that surrounds them.

"Run!" Nefari urges them, a parallel memory of her dash through these very woods with Bastian when she was a child escaping a fallen kingdom. "Run!"

Kristal takes off at a dead sprint, Beau directly behind her. The darkness enfolds them, and some of the crone's laughter breaks away from the collective and moves with them.

Nefari cannot worry about that. She can't. Not when . . .

Kristal will just have to take care of them both. She can do that. She must.

"Get ready," Vale demands as he rushes to her side, pulling his sword from its sheath. A scream sounds in the forest, but Nefari doesn't turn to it. The wraith moves closer and closer, and as it does, Nefari lets the magic grow at her fingertips until the forest brightens.

Run, Bastian! Run! She hears in her own head, the child she was to the woman she is. She wants to bolt. She wants to run.

Be brave, she hears in the delicate wind. She clamps down her jaw and widens her stance. *I will not stand in the shadow of my past.*

The wraith's cloaked body comes into full view, and Vale hurls a dagger at its head. She hadn't seen him draw it. The dagger goes right through the wraith, and the one closing in behind it. He curses. Another wraith appears behind the second. Then another.

The volume of the laughter rises.

"Now, Nefari!"

Nefari hurls her starlight at the first wraith. It shrieks and makes a popping sound as it poofs like an abrupt cloud of smoke.

"Again!"

She hurls the next one and then the next one, ignoring the sweat trickling from her neck and down her back from fear and adrenaline alone. More swarm, and she wills her body to become the starlight, to *be* starlight.

Her magic encompasses her in a blanket of bright light.

Vale covers his eyes, and she screams with all her might as she hurls the entirety of it all in the direction of the wraiths. They, too, find the fate of the first wraith.

Breathing heavily, she wills her magic to shape into the sword.

"We are hungry," a crone whispers above them. More crones cackle into the darkness. "You cannot hide from us, Princess of Light."

"Run, Vale!"

Vale listens to her, grabs her hand with his free one, and tugs her along. The light of her sword guides the way as they dash through the Shadled, the laughter following them as they do. Her heart pounds against her ribs when they hurdle fallen brittle logs, arching roots, and random boulders, nearly blind to them until they reach the obstacles themselves.

Something drops out of the trees and onto a large protruding root. They skid to a halt. *No.* Not something - *someone.*

Visible with her sword's light, the hunched crone pulls herself upright. "You cannot run, princess," she says, her voice gravelly and wicked.

"Raygelle," Vale growls.

Nefari looks behind her when she hears the thud of more crones leaping from the trees. They close in, stalking closer with their wicked, jagged teeth gleaming. Their stench surrounds them.

Regarding hair haggard and scalp balding, skin wrinkled deep, Nefari swallows at the sight of her. She looks like death reincarnated. It is said that the more dark deeds a crone does, the worse they appear.

"Do you know that you look just like your mother?" Raygelle continues, humor in her tone. She eyes the bag on Vale's shoulder. "We've waited a long time for you to

199

show your face. Even longer for you to return to your kingdom to take your crown."

"You can't have it," Nefari hisses, raising her magical sword in a threatening manner. "You'll have to kill me to get it." With that crown, they'll know who Hope-favored truly is as well as the traitor among their midst. Over her dead body will she allow them to know that a crone is the Choice-chosen, and a Salix woman is Hope-favored. She won't betray Kristal in such a devastating way.

"Oh, I don't plan to kill you, silly girl." Raygelle leans on the branch, a spider waiting to spring. "What other sort of bargaining chip would I have?"

Bargaining chip? For what? Nefari wonders. She is nobody's bargaining chip. She isn't to be gambled away because any way she looks at it, she'd wind up dead.

"Lies," Vale spits with a slash of his sword, a warning to keep her distance. "The Queen of Salix thinks she's dead. You want her to cover your own faults."

"Silence." Raygelle holds up a boney finger. "There is another reason we want her alive."

"Why?" Nefari asks, heart in her ears. "Why do you want me alive?"

"That is for us to know, and you . . . well . . ." Raygelle grins, and without a moment of hesitation, she lunges from the root. With her free hand, Nefari throws a ball of light. Raygelle veers mid-leap and clings to the bark of a

Shadled tree. Purple leaves fall and plop to the forest floor.

Raygelle hisses like a feral beast. Nefari turns to throw her magic at those behind her, but as she does, a rock plunges against her forehead. The last thing she hears before darkness descends is her name being screamed from Vale's lips.

CHAPTER EIGHTEEN

The wind is unpleasant in Kadoka. It's always unpleasant to most, but to Sibyl - to a crone - it is particularly so as she stands on the path down that mountain.

Captivated by another vision of Sindray, Sibyl waits patiently under the cover of an aged tree as the message unfolds. Sindray is at the same frozen lake with the same wolf behind her. The wolf's fur ruffles in the gale, and its eyes study Sindray, guarding her, telling to the creature's wisdom and strength.

Holding her hair at bay, Sindray peers at her reflection and quickly whispers. "A raven was sent to the factions moments ago. I told you to beware, and by this point, they'll have your princess. I will do all I can for Nefari Ashcroft and her companions, but I cannot say if I can help the one they call Kristal." Sindray gasps as a particularly rough breeze gusts snow around her. "I foresee a secret within the girl that will be dragged into

202

the light. Nefari will find out who she is if the crones haven't already. As soon as Wrenchel meets them, they will know. Wrenchel knows who Kristal is - would recognize her anywhere - just as I'm sure you might have foreseen."

Sibyl blinks in her mind's eye. She doesn't know what Sindray talks about. She knew Kristal was different, but what else had she missed?

Sibyl grumbles under her breath about the missing information.

"I may be next in line to be the leader of all factions, but it is not within my power to stop this." Sindray touches the ice and shows her a vision of Kristal. Sibyl gasps at what she sees.

There, atop Kristal's head of neatly tamed and curled brown hair, is a sparkling tiara, and behind her stands the Queen of Salix, Sieba Arsonian. The queen has dark eyes, almost pitch black, and her hand is on Kristal's shoulder, squeezing enough to cause Kristal to wince.

Together, they stand on a balcony overlooking their grey, bleak, and poverty-stricken city.

The second vision ends as quickly as it began. "I will do what I can, but I cannot promise their survival. Wrenchel wants something from your princess - your queen as I now foresee. And though I don't know what, I will send word once I find out." She glances behind her, as if hearing a sound, and quickly spits out, "Be well, my cousin. Tread lightly. They do not know you exist, and you must keep it that way. You would be the true heir, for once they find out what I am, they will kill me and replace my position with you, at all costs."

The vision ends, and Sibyl blinks and finds herself on the trail she had been taking down the mountain. She was to meet Bastian, and because of the vision, she's now late.

They have her. They have her!

The bone crier that had flown to her to deliver the message flaps its wings and soars back to the cloudy sky. Sibyl doesn't waste time. She pockets the stone and hurries her steps, slips occasionally, and descends the mountain until she reaches the busy city.

The centaurs part for her as she makes a straight path to the Council Hut. She heaves one of the double doors open, waddles quickly inside, strides past the fire and to the convening Council's Chambers. She was to be a silent witness to their discussion, but today . . .

She barges inside, and their conversation comes to a halt.

"They have her, Bastian!"

Bastian's eyes widen as he takes in Sibyl's haggard appearance. "Everyone out." No one moves, and he slams his fist on the table. The cups rattle, and some parchment flies off and floats to the floor. "Out!"

The council hastily moves away from the table, and Sibyl slides out of their way when they exit, murmuring gossip to one another. Swen is the only one to remain with Bastian. His lips are puckered as he studies her and her frantic breathing.

She balls her fingers into fists. "They have her!" she hisses.

"Slow down, young crone," Swen expresses calmly. "Who has who?"

She moves to the table and splays her fingers atop it as she leans and says through her teeth, "The crones have Nefari and Kristal." She won't tell him that she was wrong. She had been watching Nefari, but she had failed to peer into her future, to lay witness to what may happen in the coming days. She had failed. This was her fault, and -

"How do you know this?" Bastian inquires suspiciously.

Sibyl swallows as a secret is about to be spilled. "I've been in contact with the Choice-chosen."

Bastian's face darkens. "And you didn't tell me? And now we have our princess caught?" His voice rose with each word.

"Queen," she corrects. "And that is not the point. Sindray - the Choice-chosen - would not lie."

"She would, if anything but to save herself!"

Sibyl shakes her head. "The factions do not know what she is, but she is different from the rest of them. She is like me. She would not send word if - she wouldn't lie. I'd know it if she had."

"You are playing a dangerous game, Sibyl Withervein," Swen murmurs.

"But a game that must be played. Did you not hear me? They have her!"

Bastian's jaw ticks as he looks at Swen. Swen does not return the look. Instead, he presses his finger on the table's surface and proclaims, "If this is to be believed, then we must prepare to send a party to the Fades. We must retrieve the queen."

Sibyl nods frantically. "We must!"

"You want a war with the crones, Swen?"

Swen raises an eyebrow at Bastian. "Do you wish to not retrieve Fari?"

"Of course, I do! But as much as it pains me to say, she was trained for this. Waging a war against the crones - we aren't ready. We are barely recovered from the Harvest Storm. We must have faith in her."

"I won't have it," Sibyl growls. "I won't have any of it because that is not all I've learned. She is in more danger than you realize with that *person* traveling with her."

"What person?" Swen asks.

"Kristal Timpleton. She is not who she says she is."

Bastian crosses his arms. "I know you don't like her, but you should learn to. She's done nothing but aid us."

"She's the princess of Salix!" The two centaurs stiffen as if her words had struck them in the chest. Sibyl begins pacing and continues, "An Arsonian. I knew. I knew there was a darkness about the girl. More than what meets the eye. I knew! And I warned you. I warned all of you!"

"How do you know this?" Bastian asks quietly.

Sibyl slams her fist into the wall and the room shudders. "I saw it in a vision!"

Swen inches closer to Bastian. "What exactly did you see, young one?"

"I saw her with her tiara, and I saw her mother possessed by Despair. The black eyes, the sneer. She had her fingers curled into Kristal's shoulder."

"Like a threat?" Bastian's voice has a far-away quality to it, and it gives Sibyl pause.

"Perhaps," she answers truthfully. She narrows her eyes as she revisits the vision. "Yes, perhaps." But this alternative knowledge does not give her relief.

"Then, perhaps," Swen begins, his ink-stained finger pointed at her. "All is not what it seems."

"But she's still the princess of Salix," Bastian adds.

"Indeed. And if this is true . . ."

"Then, the crones will know," he finishes for Swen. "The Salix army is in their midst, and they will take her, and Nefari, back to Salix where Nefari will be hung like a prize."

"Indeed."

The conversation pauses as Bastian searches the grains of the council table.

"Now, can we send our own army to retrieve our queen?" Sibyl growls.

Bastian raises his gaze to hers. There's a dangerous edge to his expression. "Gather the Legion. We leave in an hour."

"Sir!" someone interjects from outside the door.

"Enter," Bastian calls.

The door pushes open, and a young page steps inside. He blinks at the tense scene before him, and he leaves the door open. "Someone is here to see you."

"Who?"

"He says he's from the Onyx Guard," the boy divulges, frowning.

"The Onyx Guard died the day the Shadow Kingdom was destroyed," Sibyl spits.

"He said otherwise. Said his name was - ah," the boy's face scrunches farther in an attempt to remember what he'd been told, but a man slides from the shadows of the hallway.

"Bastian," the man calls in a deep tenor. He moves into the light of the council chamber, but Bastian's expression opens with recognition.

"Ostin Rutgir," Bastian breathes.

The beautiful and sturdy man grins. "We have a problem that I think you and I have in common."

CHAPTER NINETEEN

Nefari hears her mother's voice like a whisper in the wind, *"Darkness does not dwell where there is light, Nefari. Be brave."*

With it, she's tugged from the blankness of her mind.

The carriage wheels are what fully wake Nefari, and then the bite of her cold fingers and the tip of her nose. She curls her fingers into her palms for added warmth and pries her eyes open when the carriage is jostled. Blearily, she peers around her.

"Now isn't the time to panic, Salix Blood. The guard will come for me," Vale whispers to Kristal and Beau, all three seated around her in their horse-drawn carriage prison. "Someone will come."

The planks of the carriage are made of wood, and frost clings to it. To the carriage's left and right, and front and back, long icicles droop from the ceiling's edge, some all of the way down to the planks. Metal bars cover where the ice spikes do not.

"How can you be so sure," Kristal whispers back, frosty breath billowing out of her mouth. She shivers, rubbing her arms for warmth. Nefari notes her bluish lips.

Having heard their conversation, a crone with matted hair beats against the metal bars of their cage with a wooden stick she'd been using as a cane. The cane almost strikes Kristal. She startles, slides to the side, and bumps into Vale. Vale huffs his annoyance and shoves her away from him.

With a laugh, the crone continues walking.

Nefari scoots herself into a sitting position and rubs at her aching temple. Dried blood flakes away onto her fingertips. The wound is deeper than she would have liked, and she winces at the throb it emits. She wonders just how gruesome it looks.

"Oh, thank the Divine," Beau breathes. "You're alive."

"What happened?" She peeks out between the icicles and bars. "Where are we?"

"About a three days ride from the Shadled," Vale answers. "We're almost there."

Nefari scowls at the darkening winter flatlands, great gusts of wind churning the snow and carrying it away in large vortexes. "Where?"

"To the assembly of the crone factions. I heard the others talking. All of them have gathered with the Salix Army." Vale looks at her pointedly.

"We're in the Frozen Fades," Kristal grumbles, mindful and wary of the crone with the cane still grinning wickedly at her. The crone licks her cracked lips, hungry for the taste of young flesh. "And she is going to eat me. Fari, what do we do? They took my sword."

Nefari stiffens and meets the hard stare of Vale. "The crown?"

"They have it."

Nefari snarls and searches her body for her weapons and then curses under her breath. They're all taken. She turns to the bars and gets a good look at their location. They travel on ice and a layer of snow. To her left, jutting rocks spike here and there, great structures that break up the gusts of snow. To her right is a dark forest full of snow-capped pine trees, and above her are the late evening's northern lights, the overhanging clouds glowing and freely shimmering their purple hues.

Looking behind the carriage and past the crones who follow is a familiar sight. Far in the distance, to the snow-capped Kadoka Mountains, are citizens completely unaware of their capture. What will Bastian do when he finds out they're dead? Will Wrenchel Withervein deliver her head personally? Or will she leave their bodies for the bone criers that swoop and caw over their carriage?

She looks away and groans into her hands when her head pounds at the movement of the carriage. She presses her hands to her temples once more and peers behind Vale and over the horse's rump beyond.

When she sees it, she sits up straighter, headache forgotten.

"We're here," she whispers fervently.

Ahead, many fires are lit, displaying the smoke that rises around a circle of several fat, jutting rocks - the homes of the crones. Those legends are true about the crones. It was said that the crones took these pieces of landscape and carved them into homes. The homes couldn't be much larger than Nefari's room back in Kadoka City, but they were large enough to house a few beds each.

Vale, Beau, and Kristal peer behind them when the crones hoot and holler their arrival.

The black armor of the Salix army is little specks among the ragged old crones they mingle with. Their tents circle and expand out from the crone's homes, their meager cloth flapping in the breeze. In their metal armor, Nefari isn't sure how so many have survived the harsh and unforgiving temperatures of the Frozen Fades.

"Why are they all gathered?" Nefari asks no one in particular. The three factions, each more brutal than the last, hardly ever meet in one place as far as Nefari knew.

Patrix had said that though they fall under Wrenchel Withervein's lead, they tend to not get along with their kind-hearted and lesser faction group.

From Swen, Nefari had learned that just because one crone is born into a faction, it doesn't mean they will end up there. It was recorded that Raygelle Withervein's own daughter was kicked to the lesser faction for saving a bird from one of their traps.

Nefari shivers at the thought as Vale answers, "I have no idea. Probably for you. Or the crown. Either way, they sent a raven back as soon as they knocked you out."

"And you did nothing to see me freed?" Nefari hisses.

He turns his glare on her. "What did you want me to do? Poke a crone in her eye? They took my weapons, Fari!"

"I don't want to die," Kristal whimpers. "I don't want to die!"

"You're not going to die!" Vale declares through clenched teeth. "Just keep your wits about you and your trap shut, and maybe we can live long enough to be rescued."

The crones cackle around them, having heard the warning, and the crone who had beaten against their cage says, "You wouldn't be thinking that if you knew who she really was."

Kristal swallows as all eyes fall to her.

"What does she mean?" Nefari demands as their carriage is pulled to a stop just outside the faction village.

"I - I -" She doesn't have time to answer.

Their prison is opened, and the crone with the cane tugs Nefari out. She quickly wraps chains around her wrists and then whispers a spell. "Try anything," Raygelle says, coming up behind her, "Try any of your starlight or shadow person magic, and these chains will sever your wrists."

Nefari turns to glare at her as the others are filed out. Vale and Beau get their own set of chains while Kristal is fastened with nothing but a rope.

"And if I just remove them?"

Raygelle laughs, and the others join her. "Only a crone can break that spell, young fool. How do you think the Queen of Salix keeps her shadow slaves?"

"She uses these on my people?" Both fear and anger curdle what little contents are in her grumbling stomach.

"You silly girl. How much you still have yet to learn." She crosses the distance, grabs Nefari's chains, and roughly leads her away from the carriage. The others follow obediently, passing the two black horses, who stomp their front hooves and curl their thick necks.

Ahead, crones make two lines, a space for them to walk between. As they pass through this space, murmurs are spoken. Blood is flicked from the end of long-dead weeds, and some splats against Nefari's cheek and into her hair. She doesn't flinch. She knows what this is, thanks to Dao and his knowledge.

It is said that this ritual is to cleanse the soul of good desires and fill it with darkness and death. If Nefari didn't have these chains pulling her magic from her body, she would show them what true death would look like.

As they round the rest of the carriage, Nefari nearly stops. There, waiting for her is Wrenchel Withervein. Her black cloak whips in the breeze, and her ratty hair tickles the edge of her weak jaw. Nefari would know that face anywhere, would recognize the malicious smile anywhere.

"Princess of the Shadow Kingdom. My, have you grown. Or is it queen now?" She moves her gaze to her friends, though Nefari isn't sure which one she gazes at. "Remove the bindings from the girl and return her sword," she demands. "We don't chain the Salix Royalty."

Nefari whips her head over her shoulder and watches the color drain from Kristal's face. "I'm sorry," she mouths.

She doesn't get time to process it. Kristal is led one way, and Nefari, Vale, and Beau are led another. Her mind whirls as they're guided inside a tent, crushed with the blame and shame for her friend who lied about who and what she was.

The princess. She's the princess of her enemy! The daughter!

Nefari growls when she's roughly sat in one of the tall Salix Army's tents by a particularly heavy-handed hag. Vale and Beau are given the same treatment, but Nefari can't help but feel relieved that they weren't separated.

The crones leave, and a few minutes later, Wrenchel enters, dragging Kristal along. She chucks the crown at Nefari's stomach, and Kristal winces. "Rise," she demands. Snarling, Nefari obeys, gripping the crown awkwardly in her hands. "Now, access the crown's magic."

Nefari sucks on a tooth. "No."

"Nefari, do as she wishes," Vale mumbles under his breath.

"No." Nefari shakes her head.

The boney back of Wrenchel's hand collides with her face, whipping Nefari's head to the side. The force of it drops her to her knees, and the taste of blood coats her tongue. The cold and unforgiving ground bites at her knees, but she catches herself before she falls completely over.

Nobody comments on the tent's shadows rising and curling against the roof in the shape of everyone who's inside. Nobody comments that the shadows do not obey the chains. It's a notion that Nefari tucks away.

Wrenchel steps closer to her. "You will do as I command!"

Nefari looks back at her and pulls her bleeding lip into her mouth. She tries to rise back to her feet, but Wrenchel roughly pushes her back onto her knees.

"I cannot do as you ask."

"Why?" The word is a hiss between clenched and jagged teeth.

She grins wickedly up at the Crone Faction Leader and shakes her head to free her vision of her long and tangled white hair. "Because it has no magical properties," Nefari lies. "If it had, you'd be able to access it yourself, which, I assume, you've already tried."

Nefari is glad she wasn't around for that. It would hurt to see her mother's crown - her crown - atop the enemy's head.

Snatching her hand forward as fast as a viper snake of Loess, she grips Nefari's throat, sharp nails digging into her skin. Nefari doesn't give her the satisfaction of showing fear or pain.

"I tried," Wrenchel growls. "As queen of the Shadow Kingdom, you should be able to."

"And yet, I cannot," she squeaks out. "It's just a crown, a relic, and nothing more."

Wrenchel backhands her again then snatches the crown from Nefari's grip. She roughly rights Nefari's head, slides the crown over her hair, and squints at its black stones. When nothing happens, her nostrils flare. "You will never be the queen of your people. You are weak. Pathetic. A disgrace like your mother and the soft-hearted God who gave you his useless power." Nefari's cheeks heat with raw anger. "And even if your people were free, they'd never follow you." She snatches the crown and storms out of the tent, leaving Kristal behind.

As soon as she's gone and guards are posted outside the front entrance, the only enemy remaining is Kristal. She's curled in on herself, arms crossed tightly around her middle. She moves to stand between them all, waiting for her judgment.

Bastian would have killed her by now. He wouldn't have hesitated, and if Nefari had a sword in her hand, she'd . . .

She doesn't know what she'd do. Would she strike down her friend? Or let her friend continue to suffer for what she'd done?

Beau sniffs and whispers in a small and meek voice, "I should have never left the Shadow Kingdom."

Nefari hisses and leans toward Kristal as threateningly as she can on her knees. "You're the princess!"

"I should have killed you that day in the forest," Vale growls, struggling against his chains. He sucks in a breath when they tighten around his wrists. "I should have killed you and been done with it. Did you do this? Did you tell the crones where we were and what we were doing?"

"N-N-o," she stutters.

"Then, explain how they knew," Nefari demands.

"I'm sorry," Kristal says, looking at her palms. "I didn't - I don't know how they knew. But I wanted to be free. I didn't tell you who I was because I wanted my freedom."

Nefari sits back on her heels. "And I'm supposed to believe that? Weeks we've spent together. Weeks, Kristal, and not a word! I gave you my sword, you Hope-favored piece of -"

"Quiet!" the Salix soldier guarding them shouts.

Kristal flinches at the tone of his voice. "I'm sorry."

"And your father?" Nefari carries on, ignoring the warning entirely. "Is he truly the Red Reaper? He bedded your mother, the queen?"

"Yes."

"And your sister -" Vale pauses, his face a bright and angry red. "She's the Pirate Queen. Savage Deeds is -"

"Yes," she answers with more velocity. "I cannot help who shares my blood. Please try to understand; if I could choose my family, I would. But I cannot. I can only run from them."

Nefari huffs with a curled top lip. "And now what? What will you do?"

She crosses her arms over her middle again. "They'll take me back to Salix after sunrise. They'll take me back to the castle and my mother, who may very well kill me for the company I've kept."

"You were the princess who traveled to the Fades," Vale thinks aloud, irate with himself now for not connecting the information sooner. "Tell me one thing: Why? Why were you and this army traveling to the Fades? You didn't need to come at all. It can't be for the crown. What was your reason for joining them?"

Kristal closes her eyes, but it's Nefari who slumps her posture and answers, "For a cure, and then she was going to run."

Kristal nibbles on her lip. "When I learned they planned to find shadow people to retrieve your mother's crown, I left. I wanted no part of it and would rather die than see more people suffer at the hands of my mother - at the hands of Despair. Please, believe me, I am no princess. I just have the blood of one."

Nefari raises her cold and hard stare to Kristal's. "Get out."

"But -"

"Get out, now! And do not come back or I'll wrap these chains around your throat."

Tears swell in Kristal's eyes, but she nods, turns on a heel, and exits the tent. As she leaves, the tent door is left slightly off-kilter, and through it, Nefari spies a woman standing not far away. She's discreetly trying to peer within, and somehow, Nefari feels like she's vaguely familiar. Nefari notes the scar along her face and the milky eye, which stands out amongst her beauty. But what's more noticeable is the large grey wolf who stands beside her.

"Don't worry," Vale whispers, tipping his head to the strangely gentle woman. "We know each other." His grin is mischievous and secretive, but with the guards outside, she doesn't question further.

"Wake up!" someone shouts at Patrix. He peeps open an eye and heaves himself exhaustedly off the Wench's wet-planked prison cell. He rises on unsteady feet, the ship's rocking motion much greater with the storm that rages over Widow's Bay.

He grabs the bars and peers at the pirate banging on his cell with the edge of the slop tray.

"Wick," Patrix grumbles as salty seawater splashes down the steps.

All around him, satyr slaves shout for more food, arms pushing through the space between bars or rattling their cages. He lets their voices wash over him, for anything they say or beg will not falter Wick's resolve.

"She desires ya fit as a fiddle," the pirate professes.

"Are you going to feed them, too? Or let them waste away?"

"Slaves are more entertaining when they're wasted away," he divulges, grinning. He shouts over his shoulder, "Quiet down, ya lot! Quiet, or I'll pluck yar eyeballs out!"

Sword pointed and poised to strike, Wick opens Patrix's cell gate and shoves the tray against Patrix's gut. He quickly shuts the cell door as though, at any moment, he believes Patrix would have attacked him.

Patrix has no plans to. Where would he go once he freed himself? On deck with the other pirates? Jumping overboard would be foolish. Though satyrs tend to the water of the south, they cannot swim in it. They cannot swim at all.

"Is it gold you want, Wick?" he asks him. "Jewels? What must I promise you to let me out and hide me until we get to Salix's port?"

Wick exposes decaying teeth, the wicked glee evident. "Ya won't sway me so easily, hooved man. Yar her prize."

"Whose? Luxlynn's?"

His grin broadens when footsteps slowly plod down the deck's steps. "Here, I'm addressed as Queen, or Billihook, Mr. Eiling." With the voice follow two women. One is the dark beauty Luxlynn and her large feathered hat, and the other is Yayla, who has a steel edge to her expression that Patrix hadn't witnessed on her before.

"What's the traitor doing here?" Patrix hisses. He sets his plate down and wraps his fingers around the bars to properly sneer at Yayla Misleigh. To her credit, she doesn't flinch.

Luxlynn laughs then turns to Yayla. Yayla crosses her arms over her chest when Luxlynn asks, "Do you want to tell him why? Or should I?"

The girl has the balls of an ox, Patrix will give her that, because Yayla doesn't bat an eye, nor spare an extra second for her answer. "I owed her a debt."

His grip tightens around the bars. "What kind of debt?"

She extends the set of her jaw. "To leave my family alone. She promised to keep them away from slavery in exchange for information."

Patrix's volume rises. "What kind of information?"

Luxlynn sighs contently, lovingly. "She doesn't hail from Loess, Patrix. She was born and raised in Sutherland's castle. Her family breeds the royal's horses, the ones famed across the realm."

He spits. "You were going to enslave her family? How? How could you get close enough to the Sutherland castle without -"

"I got inside the Loess's castle, didn't I? Little Yayla came to me with a bargain before her kingdom found the same fate as yours. And now, look at you. Your queen is dead, and Yayla's family gets to live."

"Another will rise in late Queen of Loess's place - in my aunt's place." Patrix hadn't had time to properly grieve his loss yet, and he can't imagine how Emory and the princess Alissia feel. And his father - he loved his sister. She was gone, and no amount of magic or wishing would bring her back.

"Her daughter?" Wick laughs as if it's a great joke.

"Perhaps." Luxlynn taps her chin. "But Yayla's debt is paid, something you would not understand. And now, a medallion will be what stands in the way of my people capturing those of her blood." She pulls a gold and aged medallion from her pocket and drops it in the waiting small and slender palm of Yayla. "Wick, escort her to the captain's quarters and see that she returns safely to shore once the storm ends. We will set sail shortly after."

"How will I get back to Sutherland?" Yayla asks.

"Another of my ships will take you."

By the elbow, Wick leads Yayla back up to the deck.

"Where, exactly, are we?" Patrix demands.

Luxlynn does not answer him. She moves closer to his cell, ignoring the murmurs from the other prisoners as if they're nothing but cattle being shipped from one country to the next. Patrix supposes that's exactly what they are.

"As for you, Mr. Eiling, she told me everything that had transpired during your visit with your father. She overheard it all. The woman you were traveling with, in the Black Market? She is the Princess of the Shadow Kingdom, long thought dead. And now, everyone will know she lives, and everyone will know the bargain you struck."

"The queen," Patrix corrects. "Nefari Astra Galazee Ashcroft is the queen. *My* queen."

"Pity," Luxlynn mocks. "Soon, she'll be dead."

The murmurs grow louder, voices carrying the words "Nefari Ashcroft lives" from one captive to the next.

His heart stops in his chest then patterns again as he inquires, "What do you mean?"

"That's right," she tips her head back and laughs at the ceiling. "You haven't heard. Wrenchel Withervein has her. In the crone's grasp, she will not live long. If she does, she'll be marched to Salix with the princess of Salix herself. She's my sister, don't you know? You guessed right, though I'm not surprised. Kristal Arsonian, what a terrible and childish name." She cocks her head to the side. "Or do you know her by Timpleton? It's hard to keep up with false names, isn't it, Trixie?"

His jaw ticks as she kisses her fingers, reaches through the bars, and presses her fingers to his lips. He has half a mind to bite her—and he would if it wouldn't cost him his tongue.

"And where are you taking me?" He already knows the answer, but he wants to hear it from her just the same. He doesn't have the heart to tell the others himself.

She crosses her arms. "I thought that was obvious."

She turns and walks to the steps, and when she's on the first step, Patrix yells, "Luxlynn!" Pausing, she tips her head to the side. "Tell me where you're taking me and the others!"

There's a moment when he's not sure if she'll answer, but the entire group collectively waits for her word. "We're near the shores of Okaton where we'll restock supplies, and then you'll be shipped to Salix. All of you will be sold as slaves."

"You're an evil wench," he growls. "I'll never know what Bastian saw in you."

She turns and walks backward up the steps. "If you think I'm anything but, then you haven't been paying attention. Think of the coin I'll get for you. The riches? The queen will pay a hefty price for the spy of the Rebel Legion." With that, she climbs the rest of the steps and disappears onto the rainy deck. "Bastian was a fool," he can hear her say, the sound nearly drowned by the rain.

"Slaves?" someone whispers.

"Get used to it, folks," he says, though it's a bad taste on his tongue. He's never been to Salix for the obvious reasons. How will he fare at the hand of Despair? For once, he doesn't have an answer.

CHAPTER TWENTY

In the tavern of Calhoun, Fawn, Dao, and Kaymen wait for Cyllian to bring their orders of ale. Outside their nearby window, snow softly falls from the evening's cloudy sky, having begun as soon as they arrived. Instead of watching it like Fawn and Kaymen are, Dao studies Cyllian. She has a grin plastered on her face while she talks to the keeper's wife. The wife fills their order behind the bar. And though Cyllian's hood hides most of her shadow features, her bright white grin doesn't go unnoticed.

The keeper's wife grins back, fills another mug, and resumes the conversation they're holding.

"You're staring at her," Fawn comments drily.

"I am not," he lies, continuing to do just that.

"You have been since we fed Deeds to the pyrens."

As soon as they arrived back to shore, they grabbed their boarded horses and sold Savage's ship to some nameless rich man. They then convinced the same man's stable boy to sell them his carriage, too, and paid for it with Savage's and the other's horses.

The boy was more than happy with the purchase, and once he left them to check on his new steeds, the four of them loaded the carriage with the big hunks of inferaze rock and covered them with thick furs. They hadn't wasted any time to head back, nor had they wasted any time in the villages that they passed, preferring to build small fires and sleep along the way in the crop fields.

To Kaymen's relief, the whole trip had been uneventful and quiet. He had anticipated wraiths or bone criers, but neither graced their straight path.

However, tonight, it was Cyllian who had argued to stop at the inn for a much-needed break, and as soon as they had their bellies full, they'd continue on to the mountains. They couldn't afford to stay any longer.

Nefari should already be back there, too. Dao looks forward to seeing her glee when they lug the inferaze into the city. But perhaps, he's not looking forward to it as much as he would have. He's changed. On this journey, he's changed, and his interests have shifted from a princess who did not want him to a healer whose eyes sparkled every time she talked with him.

"What of it?" Dao slumps back into his chair and traces the grain of the table's wood.

Kaymen pitches forward and whispers, "She's been in love with you since the moment we were escorted to Kadoka City."

Dao frowns. "She has not."

"He speaks the truth," Fawn says, smirking. She crosses her arms over her chest and bumps her shoulder against his. It nearly knocks him off his stool.

A tray is set on the counter by the wife, and their ale and meat pies are stacked upon it. Gently, Cyllian picks it up and heads back to them, tray balanced perfectly in both hands. He's never noticed how steady her hands are, but he supposes as a healer, she must possess such a skill.

Kaymen quickly whispers, "Fawn and I have bets of your union. Don't disappoint me."

Dao would have smacked him if Cyllian wasn't watching. Wind rattles the window, and Dao shivers as a drafty tendril curls around his cloak and dips into his hood. Or maybe he shivers because he knows Fawn and Kaymen are right.

As she places the tray on the table and slides into her seat, Dao catches the troubled set of her eyes. He pitches forward, hooking a finger in his mug's handle. "What is it?"

"Rumors." Cyllian's eyebrows pinch together, and she shivers and rubs at her arms. "I overheard some of the patrons talking at the bar," she whispers then raises her gaze to meet Dao's.

"And?" He sips and lets the warm ale wash over him. Rumors. More rumors. This realm was full of them, and in a little village like this, they're plentiful. "What did they have to say?"

She touches her chin, fingers trembling against her skin. "They said that pirates had invaded Loess."

The group's expressions go blank, Kaymen's mug lifted halfway to his mouth. "What of their queen?" he asks.

"Dead." She swallows thickly. "And her nephew was taken."

"Is this nephew important?" Fawn wonders aloud, picking at the crust of her meat pie. Steam rises where the pie is opened, and it brings the delicious scent to Dao's nose.

"The nephew is known to be friends of many kingdoms."

Dao steals a chunk of crust that had broken away from Fawn's pie and pops it into his mouth. He ignores Fawn's murderous stare and inquires, "Who is this nephew?"

"I don't know, but the queen's last name is Eiling, Dao. They said so. I heard them."

Fawn pauses chewing. "Eiling . . ."

She nods, and in an even muffled voice, she whispers, "I think it safe to assume who the nephew is."

Silence stretches across the table. Silence and still postures.

"Act normal," Kaymen orders them softly. Some of the patrons have noticed their unusual stiffening that teamed with their hidden appearances. To anyone else, they'd look like trouble.

To appear as such, Dao brings the mug to his lips and washes down the crust. *Patrix.* Patrix was taken by the very pirates who desire him dead. And in their hands, and with a little torture, he could be deadly.

Inside his own mug, Kaymen continues, "What do you want to do, Dao?"

Dao isn't sure when he became their group's leader, but he answers honestly. "Nothing."

"Nothing?" Cyllian hisses.

"Nothing." With trembling hands, he pulls his own meat pie to him. "We will do nothing. Saving Patrix isn't up to us. He'll have to care for himself until we talk to Bastian."

"They'll sell him, Dao," Fawn murmurs under her breath. "He's Luxlynn's prize. She will sell him to the highest bidder, and that bidder will be the Queen of Salix."

Dao looks around the tavern. The collective's attention had turned back to their ale and company. "He is not a child. He will find a way to endure it. There's nothing we can do for him. The four of us - there's nothing we can do."

Cyllian roughly scoots back her stool. The wooden legs squeal against the floor. "I'll see you in the stables," she angrily snaps.

Fawn makes to follow her out the door, but Dao grabs her arm. "Let her stew it over. Eat up. We will send a raven to Sibyl and make her aware of the situation, but you can't deny what I said. Patrix is on his own."

With a flex of her jaw, Fawn nods and reluctantly digs into her steaming meat pie.

Dao watches the door close behind Cyllian and the snow that pushes inside, now melting against the floor. She's mad, and she has the right to be, but he can't help but wonder what sort of situation he'll find himself in regarding whatever was blossoming between himself and Cyllian. He has a sinking feeling that he just destroyed it all with those simple words of truth. Cyllian is too soft - too kind to see it, to understand. Perhaps, when they arrive home, Sibyl will reassure her that they made the right move.

Before they can finish their meal, Cyllian returns, her eyes wider than they had been before. "Nefari and Kristal . . ."

Dao stands, "Are they back?" He had assumed they'd be in Kadoka by now.

She shakes her head. "Astra and Joana are still stabled."

He nearly chokes on his bite of food. They should have returned before them. "Eat, we have to leave. We need to get back to the city, now!"

Kaymen stands with him. "Shouldn't we travel to the Shadow Kingdom?" he asks under his breath.

"No." Dao takes one more bite and moves his stool hastily. "If they're not back by now, something went wrong. Grab their horses, Cyllian. We're leaving."

"But Dao-" Fawn begins.

"We have to leave, and we cannot leave their horses behind. Something is wrong, Fawn. Something is wrong, and we have to get back to Sibyl before we can do anything else about our friends, do you understand?"

She grinds her teeth and follows Cyllian quickly out of the taverns.

"Crones are in that forest, Dao," Kaymen says softly as he strides out the door with Dao and into the snow.

"Exactly," he growls. Because if they aren't back yet, they're either dead or taken. He isn't sure which fate is worse.

CHAPTER TWENTY-ONE

A gust of wind is what wakes Nefari from her sleep. For a moment, she's disoriented about where she is, but when she sees Vale and Beau startle awake in front of her from across a small and meager fire, it all comes crashing back.

Come this morning, they will be marched to Salix. Come this morning, Nefari will be a true slave.

A crone had entered their tent, bringing in the morning rays and cold breeze when she opened the tent door. Her gentle grace as she strides inside doesn't go unnoticed, nor does the leather pack slung over her shoulder and the bright torchlight in her hand.

She's different from the others. Kinder, even. Nefari can tell just by her gait and unhunched shoulders.

She stops by the ash of the fire and surveys the factions' prisoners with a sobering expression.

Nefari sits up and rubs her eyes with the back of her hands and then squints as she focuses on the crone's features. It's the crone she had seen peering into the tent - the one with the wolf and the puckered scar. Nefari looks behind her to see the wolf through a crack in the tent's door, the eyes as sharp and intelligent as any human's. Amid the snow, it watches the tent with alert interest.

She also catches the glimpse of the glinting armor belonging to a Salix soldier who guards their captives. This crone must be trusted by the army if she was allowed entrance without questioning.

"Who are you?" Nefari asks.

"Sindray Withervein," Vale murmurs. "Niece of Wrenchel."

Withervein, Nefari thinks to herself. Does Sindray know about Sibyl's existence? Wrenchel is her grandmother, after all. Sibyl would be her cousin, twice removed. She would have been old enough to remember Sibyl's mother's pregnancy. Nefari wonders what happened to Sibyl's mother because she hadn't yet been introduced to Wrenchel's daughter.

Sindray presses her finger to her lips and softly sets down the pack. She passes the torch to Vale who grabs it awkwardly due to his chains. The chains are biting into his wrists, and little red marks mar the skin.

"Vale," she returns the greeting. "Keep your voices down. These walls are parchment-thin."

And doesn't Nefari know it? All night she battled with freezing limbs.

"We know," Beau says, shivering.

Frowning, Nefari whispers, "How do you two know each other?"

"Remember when I first found you in the alley? Remember when I said the Rebel Legion isn't the only one who has a crone on their side?"

Nefari nods. "She's the one?"

Vale inclines his head. "We met by accident once. I found her on the iced pond with her wolf, walking across it without a care in the world."

Sindray grins a small smile as she passes Nefari salve for her cut lip. Nefari hastily applies it as Sindray explains, "He hunted me. I know about your crone, so there is no need to hide it from me. Her mother was one who died in your mother's blast, a cold-hearted wench that outmatched Wrenchel's desire to see blood spilled with every encounter she made."

Nefari's fear must have been present on her face because Sindray adds, "There is no reason to be frightened of me. Secrets are something I've become adept at keeping. Yours is safe with me."

239

Still stuck on the previous topic, Vale mocks, "I only hunted you for a moment."

"That is not how I remember it. I remember a few daggers aimed for my head. And being chased across a frozen pond until my wolf threatened your life."

"'What are you doing in here," Nefari pushes.

"Here," she says, moving on from the conversation entirely. She digs a loaf of bread from the pack, splits it in three, and passes it to them. It's the first meal they've received, and they bite into it gratefully. "Eat and gather your strength. Quickly, we don't have much time."

"Until the march to our slavery?" Nefari asks around a mouthful of food.

Sindray meets her gaze. "For your escape to freedom." She pulls two pitch-black wool cloaks from her pack, the ones the crones wear. The stench coming off them is unmistakable. "The crown," she whispers, showing them a peek of its glistening black stones from within her pack. "We don't have long before they discover it's missing."

"How did you get it in your grasp in the first place?" Beau inquires, leary despite Vale's validation. It's a valid question, one Nefari had been wondering herself.

Sindray smirks, and the expression tugs on her scar. Vale answers for her, "Because she's the leader of the lesser faction and heir to all factions."

"I thought Raygelle was heir," Nefari asks, frowning when Sindray passes both her and Beau each a cloak. Since Sibyl's mother is dead and they believe Sibyl to be dead, then the likely candidate would be Wrenchel's sister.

Sindray shakes her head. "No. Raygelle has no desire to take her sister's place should her sister fall, be it by old age or by sword. She passed the title to me in my youth." She looks thoughtfully at the crown. "Does it work?"

Nefari shoves the last bit of bread into her mouth and passes her back the salve. "Does what work?"

"The crown." She touches one stone then frowns at the two missing ones. "Does it show you who the Divine are?"

Nefari glances at Vale, a wordless question to see if he still has the stone. He subtly nods, and Nefari breathes a sigh of relief. To Sindray, she asks, "Why should I tell you?"

Slowly, Sindray lifts her gaze to Nefari. "Because I have just as much to lose as you do should this crown be accessed by anyone but the Fate-blessed, Choice-chosen, or Hope-favored. Should it get into the hands of the Despair-born . . ."

"The Despair-born?" Beau interrupts, having finished her bread, too.

"The queen of Salix," Nefari answers. She says to Sindray, "Why? What do you have to lose?"

"She is the Choice-chosen, Nefari," Vale whispers, barely a breath.

Nefari blinks. And then blinks again. She remembers the skull of omen's prophecy with perfect clarity. *Born to have a heart as black as coal, the Choice-chosen's purity will have unending pull. A heart so gold is foretold, hidden in places where there's nothing but cold. She will be the sympathizer of both enemy and kin, a shield for those shackled and sold. And with the wolf as a guide, she will choose to stand by those who wished they had died.*

"You're . . . the wolf - it's in your -"

"I am her, and make no mistake; they will kill me for it once it comes to them that the wolf I have is the one the prophecy speaks of. Now, please. Put on the cloaks. We don't have much time."

Nefari wonders if 'we' is meant for all of them or just for her.

Vale surveys himself. "What am I to wear?"

"After all this time, do you truly think so little of me?" Sindray's eyebrows raise chastisingly for thinking she hadn't thought ahead. Without taking her eyes off Vale, she whistles.

The guard outside stirs while Sindray makes her way to the front of the tent, tucking herself into a corner right next to the flapping door. The guard dips inside, hand on sword, and just as he does, Sindray whispers a spell. The words are quick and rough, of a language long since dead according to Swen Copsteel's assurances. It is a language the crones used to speak before the common tongue had spread across the realms back when the fee still roamed.

The spell snaps his neck before he can utter a word. He falls to the floor in a heap of clattering armor.

Sindray crouches next to him and starts undressing his armor. "Help me," she demands of Vale. Vale scrambles to his feet and replaces Sindray's maneuverings, undoing straps and sliding armor off of limbs.

Rushing to her back, Sindray frantically digs inside. "You should have everything here for a few days' walk. Once you leave this tent, you must hurry. Do you understand?"

Adrenaline pumps through Nefari's body, both fear and exhilaration for what they're about to do. Some of the fear of this crone herself and what she had done to the guard. But instead of dwelling on it, Nefari and Beau quickly nod. A spell like that could destroy anyone. A spell like that . . .

"Good." Sindray holds out her hands. "Give me your wrists."

Nefari obeys, her chains clinking quietly. Hovering her hands above the metal, Sindray murmurs more magic, solely different from the one she just used. Nefari studies her as she does, wary and uncertain. How had Sindray learned this magic? Had it come from Choice when he gave himself to her? Does she remember when that day had occurred? Nefari has so many questions, none that will be answered for her today.

The chains fall to the ground just like the guard had. She moves to Beau while Nefari rubs at her sore wrists, gathers herself to her feet, and hastily fastens the cloak around her neck. She flips the hood up then moves across the tent to help Vale.

As soon as all of the armor is free and Vale's chains are removed, all three women help him put on the armor, hastily strapping and fastening. Then, he takes the man's sword and passes Beau the dagger that was strapped to the soldier's hip.

"Can you use your magic if the need arises?" Sindray asks.

"Of course I can," Nefari spits, though she knows it may bring the wraiths.

"Good," she says again. "The wraiths do not come this far north, for they cannot fly in such cold environments and do not wish to test the crone's magic, but do not count on it. Once you hit the Fade's deeper forests, they will be roaming if you use it again."

"Okay. Are we ready?" The three make to leave the tent, but Nefari turns to Sindray, who passes them the pack. "Thank you, for all you've done. I - Thank you."

"You would do the same for me, this I know." Sindray taps her temple, inclines her head, and hesitates. "You know, the princess of Salix - the Hope-favored - loves you as her own flesh and blood. She's been trying to negotiate your release since you arrived, though they know nothing of her Divinity. They marched her off before breakfast just to be rid of her begging. If she betrayed you, it wasn't to break your heart but to free her own. She has hope, Fate-blessed. She has hope even though she's gone back to the hell she escaped from."

"Sindray," Vale warns when color splashes across Nefari's cheeks. "Perhaps we'll have this discussion another time?"

She's gone. Kristal is gone.

In truth, in some deep part of herself that isn't tainted with rage and betrayal, Nefari believes Sindray, knows she speaks the wisdom of a hard life, being kind-hearted in factions so brutal. But she can't think about Kristal at this moment. She can't think about her being in the hands of Despair once more. At this moment, Nefari, Vale, and Beau's freedom are all that matters, for if Nefari is not free, she cannot free her people, both those harvested and those not. Kristal and Kristal's freedom is low on her list because these shards of her broken life are cutting deeper than glass, and some of those shards

245

were made by the Princess of Salix. The fresh wounds they've caused cannot be so easily forgiven.

"Indeed," Sindray agrees, considering Nefari carefully with her one good eye. "I will find you when I can, and hopefully, others will choose to join me, but I must bide my time and wait for the right moment."

"I'd expect nothing less," Vale says, touching her shoulder.

"But, one more thing, Nefari. You never answered me. Does the crown work?"

Nefari wets her lips. "It does."

She nods in small successions. "Go. Hurry. Right now, they're distracted, but they won't be once it's time to retrieve you for the trek back to Salix. Be well, Queen of Shadows, for your future is as harrowing as your past."

Nefari doesn't know what to make of her words of wisdom, doesn't know if she should take it as a threat or take it as a warning for her own well-being. But she asks none of these things. Instead, the three of them dip out into the morning air, feeling the cold biting at their skin.

Cloaks pulled over their heads, they make their way through the snow blowing across the landscape and the throng of the army who faces the village. The army awaits breakfast while they engage in normal posturing with the usual pecking order jokes and shoves. Nefari doesn't know who would have the energy to do such things in cold environments, but at least, the harvested shadow people remain unmoving.

As they pass a cluster of the harvested, they tuck their cloaks tightly around them. She has the desire to peek at them, to see if there's any life within, but she doesn't.

"This way," Vale urges them. They follow his lead, weaving in and out of lines, all none-the-wiser.

Once they make it through the crowd, they hustle toward the trees.

When they're nearly alone and far enough away from the collective, Nefari demands under her breath, "Why didn't you tell me you knew who she was - who the Choice-chosen was! You had -"

"Because it was for her protection! Just like I protected you."

Nefari huffs. She'd pick this fight once they were clear and safely in the cover of the woods.

Beau trips on an icy rock. She falls to the snow and scrambles for the dagger which had flung a few feet away. Vale curses under his breath, grips her elbow, and brings her upright. Nefari snatches up the dagger and passes it to Beau.

"Sorry, sorry," she murmurs, sticking her dagger into her cloak pocket. "There was ice and I-"

"It doesn't matter. We have to hurry." He leads them around jutting ice. "This way."

"Hey!" someone shouts behind them, the voice nearly carried away in the harsh wind. "Hey, you! Stop! Stop!"

Vale grabs both their elbows, and they begin to rush, causing their cloak hoods to fall from their heads the faster they move. They run as fast as they can, hurdling small spikes of ice and dashing around large drifts of snow.

"Do you know your way through the forest?" Nefari asks, heart thumping loudly in her chest. She hears the Salix man shouting to the others as soon as they hit the tree line and dip inside.

"I've lived in these forests," he explains breathlessly, in adrenaline or exertion, Nefari isn't sure. "We head south where the trees are thicker. That's where we'll find the Onyx Guard."

He skids to a halt and places his arms out to stop both women.

Nefari lifts her gaze and finds a small Salix army unit with dead deer slung over a few of their shoulders, and bows over the other. Vale pulls his borrowed sword from its sheath, and the group drops their burdens at his wordless threat.

"Well, well," one of them says, stepping closer. Ice crunches under his boot.

"It would appear we have a couple of escapees," taunts another.

"Leave, pretend you never saw us, and I'll let you live," Vale growls.

"Vale," Nefari warns, gripping his shoulder. There's a dozen of them. How are they to cut them down when there's an army chasing them from behind?

A horn sounds in the distance, and Nefari's heart skips a beat to the familiar sound. She recognizes the horn and would know that warning anywhere.

Another horn joins the first. And then another until the Fades are echoing the sweet song of war.

"The Rebel Legion," Nefari breathes.

CHAPTER TWENTY-TWO

"Are you sure?" Vale murmurs under his breath.

"Yes!"

The shouts of the coming army turn away, and new shouts about readying bows replace it.

The group before them lifts their heads, confused about the sound. They've never met the Rebel Legion, for all those of Salix blood who have, have never survived.

Unsteadily, they pull their swords from their sheaths as one, and Vale crouches, preparing himself. "Stay behind me."

Nefari steps back but protests, "By the Divine, Vale." He can't take on this many. She's never met a warrior who could, aside from Bastian. Vale is no centaur.

"Do what I say!"

Shakily, Beau pulls her dagger from underneath her cloak, and when they rush, Nefari lets the light hum around her fingertips. She can't let him do this alone.

The magic comes faster than it had in the Shadow Kingdom, ready and waiting, having been shackled as much as Nefari had. Her skin turns black, and stars speckle every inch. She grips both Vale and Beau's shoulders, and with a shove to the shadows, they travel from one tree's shadow to another tree's shadow behind the group.

Vale immediately pops through and plunges his sword into the first man's back. Then the next. Blood coats the ground, and while it does, Nefari shapes her magic, raising her sword made of starlight. It gleams like the sun. It gleams like the ice spread out before them. It gleams like her skin, the skin of her people.

Her people. These men are an extension of who is to blame for her people's conditions.

She hollers and darts forward. Before one particular soldier can swing his sword, she cuts him down. Her sword slices like butter, and burning flesh stings her nose. She pays no mind to it.

Beyond, the volume of the shouts of the Rebel Legion clashing with the crones rises into the morning sky, but Nefari remains concentrated, focused, working side by side with Vale.

She twirls and slashes, crouches, and plunges her blade until her arms, her neck, her body is covered in the blood of her enemy. Bone criers caw about their heads, circling, waiting, having smelled the fresh blood and flown from the trees like the dead woken from their grave.

A soldier parries his sword just in time. It sizzles when it meets Nefari's starlight, and her sword cuts right through it. The tip clatters to the ground, and Nefari meets his frightened stare. She grins and whirls. His head tumbles to the ground right next to it.

She continues to fight, hollering and grunting when she must. All of her anger, all of her frustration at being lied to time and time again, she puts it into her skill, into her swiftness, and when the last one is cut down, she spins to find another, breathing heavily.

But there isn't another. There isn't anyone left to fight. Around her lay the dead.

Vale lifts his gaze to meet hers. He's just as bloody as she is, but there's a cut on his arm. She releases her starlight sword, and it disappears.

Rushing to him, she grabs his arm and examines the wound. "How deep is it?"

He slowly takes back his arm. "I'll live." He peers past her and squints at the trees and the gusts of snow as though he can see through them to where the army is fighting the Rebel Legion. "Should we?"

"No. We have the crown, Vale. We have to leave and leave quickly."

"But what if they don't survive?" Beau asks. They both look at her. She's trembling like a leaf in the wind, her dagger bloodless and pointed to strike.

Nefari turns to her and gently takes the dagger by the hilt. "They'll survive." She grabs her now empty hand and would have tugged her along if there wasn't a hunched and haggard woman waiting in their path.

"Wrenchel," she hisses. She should have known Wrenchel would be on their tail. She should have anticipated it, and unfortunately, she's not alone.

Nefari throws the dagger to meet Wrenchel's eye, but Wrenchel veers in the last split second.

"I can smell blood a half-mile away, girl," Wrenchel proclaims as the dagger slides across the white and slippery forest floor and plunges into a drift. The crones behind her are silent pillars. "The crown is ours. We've waited. We've watched. We need it."

Nefari looks at the pack on Beau's shoulders. "Why? Why do you need it? Why do you need me?"

Wrenchel tips her head one way then the other. "We need the crown to find the other Hope-favored and

Choice-chosen, and though the queen believes she has Hope-favored in her dungeons, she is absolutely wrong. We want to keep her ignorant. Finding the Choice-chosen is a task bestowed to us by the queen, and if we do not fulfill it, we are all dead. We'll be lucky if she doesn't kill us for learning of your existence, but if she were to learn she does not have the Hope-favored, the realm would feel her wrath." She tucks her chin, forehead pointing at Nefari. Her hands flex at her sides. "And as for you, I think you've outlived your usefulness. You are a burden just like your friend, and I, for one, cannot wait to see what she does with your corpse."

"What friend?" *Keep her talking,* Nefari says to herself. *Stall! Find a way out!* A unit of soldiers is one thing. A group of crones is another.

"A raven has already been sent from Luxlynn Billihook. Did you know she has your dear friend, the spy? Do you know the spy was tailed by another spy, and now everyone you fear knows you're alive?"

Nefari sucks in a breath but does not respond in any other way.

"Ha! I thought not! The Queen of Salix will know you're alive, and she'll want your head. You'll travel to Salix where she can put it on a spike, but not before I get what I want. Now! Give me that crown!" She leaps for Beau, but Nefari shoves her shoulder into the crone midair. The crone flies to the side and lands on all fours. She hisses like a feral cat.

"I won't let you have it!" Nefari wills the starlight sword to return. The shadows bend toward her, pulled from the trees and the shadows of those around her.

Wrenchel rights herself with a wicked gleam in her eye. "Do you know what happened to your mother while you hid?"

"She died trying to save me," Nefari spits.

"Bah!" she swipes a hand through the air. "All she wanted was a prophecy. She put everything at risk for the prophecy."

More crones join Wrenchel's group, one of them Sindray. Sindray discreetly inclines her head to Nefari. To anyone else, the action would appear defensive. In the short time Nefari had been in her company, she recognized the girl truly had the gold heart Sibyl's fate card showed her, and not the black heart of all the others. She's good, and her magic is great. Perhaps greater than the others gathering around them.

Vale moves to guard Beau, one arm held out in front of her. Nefari and Wrenchel start to circle one another, one crouched and the other hunched.

Faction leader against princess. Age against youth.

Eyes sparking with humor, Wrenchel continues, "She knew we had a prophecy that belonged to you, and she desired to hear it. It was first spoken by Sindray, along with the crown's properties. And in exchange for our

255

knowledge, your mother unknowingly showed us the very crown you now protect. We've been trying to find it ever since."

"And you failed. You needed the people you helped enslave to get it."

"An unfortunate oversight. You see, we could not find it when the Harvest Storm unfolded to perfection. That night, she had stowed it away. And when my sister went looking for you, she first stopped at your mother's chambers and destroyed it looking for that crown. But it was lost anyway, just like you were. We couldn't find it, nor you, and we ran before we too became ash in our own making."

"You couldn't have it then, and you can't have it now. You'll have to go through me."

Patronizingly, Wrenchel confesses, "I think we can manage. Royal flesh is not something we've tasted in a long, long time. Perhaps once we are finished with you, we will hunt Kristal along the beaten path to Salix."

"Do not touch her," Nefari growls.

A nameless crone tosses her sword at Wrenchel, and Wrenchel catches it on the blade's side. The blade cuts into the hag's palm, and she shows no signs of pain as she squeezes. Blood wells and drips past her wrist, splatting against the snow by Wrenchel's boots. "Do you have a sore spot, Nefari Astra Galazee Ashcroft, the pathetic Queen of the Shadow Kingdom?"

And Nefari isn't sure why she says it, but she can't help but feel some kind of kinship to the girl who had betrayed her. "If you touch her, I will kill you myself. I will kill you, Wrenchel." She shouldn't be defending her. She shouldn't but . . .

"Isn't that why we are circling one another? One will die, and one will live. You don't get it, do you?" she adds with a cackle. "You cannot outmatch us. You cannot save yourself or your friends or your lover. They will die today, and you'll head to Salix where you belong, shackled to your last life."

With that, she runs at Nefari, sword raised high above her head.

CHAPTER TWENTY-THREE

Nefari dodges the first blow, but she doesn't anticipate the next. Wrenchel's sword slides against her shoulder. She shouts as pain seeps across the fresh wound. Stumbling back a few steps, she clutches the fresh wound. Despite her age, the crone is fast. Too fast.

Nefari stares at her fingers as Wrenchel laughs, tasting the air with a flick of her tongue. "Such lovely blood."

Nefari lifts her gaze to the hag, anger boiling in the pit of her gut. "You are the reason my mother is dead!" She whips her blade, but Wrenchel ducks. "You are the reason my kingdom is ash!" Another slash. Wrenchel's hair is caught, fizzled, and sizzled. A lock of the ragged gray hair falls to the ice.

Wrenchel watches it and licks her lips. "That was your own queen's fault," she growls. Nefari sucks in a breath when Wrenchel kicks her in the gut. At the surprise of it, her sword pops from her hand and winks out before it hits the snow.

She falls on her rump, and Wrenchel pounces, landing on top of her. Nefari brings up her arms to shove the crone off, but with Wrenchel's free hand, she grabs Nefari's wrists and pins both to the ground. Nefari growls her anger and tries to wiggle free, but the crone is strong and heavy.

"Get up, Nefari!" Vale shouts. His words go unheard.

"You do not get to blame me for your mother's faults. You leave that lie with your mother's ashes."

Nefari takes a quick glance around her, noting how Vale and Beau are now restrained by the crones. The bag with the crown is held in one of their hands. *Sindray's* hands.

When her haze rises to Sindray's, she finds tears gathered in her eyes. Sindray blinks as good as any confirmation. *The crown. She has the crown and -*

With her attention diverted elsewhere, Wrenchel releases her wrists to take her sword and stab it into Nefari's shoulder above the collarbone.

Nefari screams.

"Your mother was weak, just like you. You have the magic of the Divine, yet you do nothing with it, you fool. You do nothing but tramp around and call yourself the Queen of Shadows. You are no queen. You're not half of what your mother was."

"Shut up! Shut up!" Nefari shouts. She's never wanted it—either of them—her title, her fate. She's never wanted to be Fate itself, nor to be the queen, but someone must. Someone has to. And she'll do it. Wrenchel's words tickle Nefari's self-consciousness just the same. Maybe she won't. Maybe she is half the queen she ought to be.

"Get up, Nefari!" Vale yells again, but the sound is distant in Nefari's mind. "You cannot listen to her! You are the queen! And a queen fights! Your mother fought! You have to fight!"

Resolve couples with Nefari's rage, and the nearby shadows quiver in the gushing gales of snow. Out of the corner of her eye, she sees Sindray's attention stray to it. A small smile tips up her lips.

"I will not be silent!" Wrenchel presses the finger into the outer edges of her wound and brings the blood to her lips. She squeezes Nefari's legs with her thighs as she says, "I taste it. The finest of wines mixed with honey and lemon. I can taste fate cross my tongue, and I wonder, dear Nefari, what it is you have that I don't. You have it! And you do nothing with it, just like your mother. You do nothing to see your people to the safety of your kingdom. You do nothing to right your mother's wrongs."

The tip of a short hidden blade strapped to Wrenchel's thigh digs into Nefari's hip. When warmth spreads across the skin of her hip, she knows blood has been drawn.

Tears spring to Nefari's eyes. "She didn't do anything wrong!" And she hadn't. This Nefari knew when the Harvest Storm invaded Kadoka City.

"She did! There were so many things she could have done. So many avenues she could have taken, but she chose none of them. She chose death. And do you know why, little girl?" Nefari tries to squirm free under Wrenchel, but the blade in her shoulder causes her to shout. It's embedded in the ice at Nefari's back. "She chose it because she believed it would give you the strength to do what you must."

What I must, Nefari thinks to herself. Does Wrenchel speak the truth? What had she done? Though she had chosen to pick up her crown, what had she planned to free her people, aside from the inferaze? She had no plan. She had no avenue. She had nothing but the ash and blood and sweat and tears of her people.

Be brave, the breeze whispers. *Be brave.*

Nefari grinds her teeth and glares through bleary eyes up at Wrenchel. She has been brave. That is what she has. She has the bravery of her mother and all those before her. By picking up her crown, she had been brave.

I will not stand in the shadow of my past.

Through sheer will and a clamped jaw, she pushes herself up the blade until she's in Wrenchel's face.

261

Wrenchel's eyes are wide, shocked. "Be brave, Wrenchel Withervein, for this will hurt."

The shadows flare.

She quickly grabs the short blade from Wrenchel's thigh and stabs Wrenchel in the back. As Wrenchel rears with a pain-filled shout, Nefari pulls the sword from her shoulder with a scream of her own.

"Yes!" Vale hollers. "Yes! Get up, Nefari!"

"Now!" Sindray demands, and for a moment, Nefari thought she was talking to her, but behind Vale and the others, a wolf leaps from the trees. The wolf tackles a crone to the ground, teeth clamped around the woman's throat. The crone screams and gurgles, and Nefari uses the distraction to call upon the leaping shadows who bend willingly toward her like living things. They detach from their trees, from the crones, and move toward Wrenchel. She wails when they surround her, waves her hands as if to bat them away.

Heart pounding in her ears, breaths heavy, blood dripping down her chest, she then commands Wrenchel's shadow with the will of a single thought. Wrenchel's shadow detaches itself from the ground and grabs Wrenchel by the throat.

"Get them away! Get them away!" Wrenchel chokes out, flinging her arms in every direction. Nefari throws her off of her, but Wrenchel pays no mind as she scrambles in the snow. Her arms pass through the shadows as though they're nothing but wind.

Nefari doesn't hesitate. She stands, drops Wrenchel's blade, and calls upon her own. Then, with one deep exhale, she plunges the sword into Wrenchel's chest.

Wrenchel stops moving, clutches the sword, and gasps for breath. Where her hands touch, smoke rises. Her skin burns away until the sword meets the bones of her palm. "You - I-"

"Are mine," Nefari hisses in her face. "I told you to be brave, Wrenchel. Will you die with tears in your eyes? Will you be weak?"

"I - am - not -" Wrenchel says, the words cut off with the last gush of air. Her eyes lull to the sky, and the shadows that had been surrounding her return to their given places.

Nefari whirls, sword poised for retaliation, but the wolf attacks the next crone. That's not what Nefari watches, however. Nor does she watch the next crone he attacks.

Sindray's free hand is raised in front of the others, and in the breeze, Nefari hears whispers. Whispers she cannot make out.

"What are you doing?" Nefari asks her, stepping forward. The other crones have their own hands clamped over their ears, groaning and moaning.

"You're not the only one with god-like magic," Sindray declares to her.

Vale crosses the distance to Nefari with Beau in tow. "She's giving them visions, a choice between the darkness or her side."

"And if they choose the darkness?" Nefari watches as the crones writhe to whatever Sindray is showing them.

"Then, they die."

Sindray's voice carries like that of a god she truly represents, white light shimmering across her skin. "Make your choice."

"We will never follow you!" one hisses.

"Choice-chosen, filth!" spits another.

Their voices are coupled with the shouts of the dying battle still raging on the other side of the trees.

Those who say nothing kneel to one knee, ears still covered with pained expressions etched across their faces. Sindray twists her wrist and snaps the neck of the two who protested against her. She then blows out a breath, and the whispers stop, but not before one swirls around Nefari.

"Be brave," it says in her mother's voice.

Nefari gasps and steps backward. "You - The voice was always you."

CHAPTER TWENTY-FOUR

Nefari cannot believe it. Doesn't want to believe it. All the whispers she heard, she had thought they were her mother. She hadn't thought them to be anything but a memory that constantly invaded her mind when choices were hard - when her life was hard. But here, the answers lie.

Sindray spares Nefari only a glance before she turns back to the group, now peering up at her in wonder. "Wrenchel is dead. As heir, you will follow me."

It doesn't take long for them to bow in the snow though slowly with slight sneers that expose sharp and jagged teeth. The half-hearted, begrudging show of respect does nothing for Nefari. She wonders what Sindray thinks on the matter but refrains from asking.

"If there are any crones left," Sindray adds. "Tell them once this is over. Tell them what transpired here today, and make no mistake; any who disobey will find the same fate as our sisters." She doesn't have to gesture to the dead, but the crones look to them anyway.

The last of the sounds of battle fade, and the crones gather themselves to their feet, wordlessly walk toward the line of trees, and raise their hands in surrender as they disappear through them. In Nefari's opinion, they deserve worse fates than what a complete surrender will offer, but she turns her attention to the more pressing matter.

"It was you," Nefari growls, balling her fists at her sides. "You've been the voice who told me to be brave. You've borrowed my mother's voice."

Sindray slowly turns to face her. Exhaustion has settled in the set of her eyes. "It was me," she confesses, bending to adjust the cloak of a dead crone with a loving affection the crone doesn't deserve.

"Why!" Her voice booms, and the trees and shadows shudder.

She rises and exhales deeply. "Because someone had to remind you who you are. Someone had to remind you who you're meant to be."

Nefari snarls. It was an invasion of privacy. It was words built on a lie. It was - it was exactly what she needed to hear, time and time again.

"What did you show them?" Beau asks.

Sindray raises her gaze and looks at Beau. She hands the bag with the crown to Vale as she says, "Their own deaths."

Thoroughly done with the death and the lies and deceit, Nefari storms past Sindray and through the very trees the crones had disappeared through. Sindray and Vale watch her go, but Beau follows her.

"Nefari, wait," Sindray calls. She ignores her.

"She never meant you harm, Nefari," Beau eventually whispers as they tread through the snow.

"I know."

"Then why are you so upset?"

They push through the last bit of trees and halt in their steps. Centaurs walk from dead body to dead body, some checking pulses and others taking the life of those who still gasp for it. A few centaurs are mixed within the death, and Nefari whispers, "This is why."

The ice towers that had jutted to the sky are now crumbled to the ground, and to the left is a crowd of crones, forced to kneel among the rubble. None of the Salix army survived, harvested or not.

"And could this have been avoided?"

"No," she begrudgingly answers.

Sibyl Withervein taps her finger on her table and observes both Cyllian and Dao seated across from her. They fidgeted with untold feelings, feelings that slither across Sibyl's skin like sticky oil.

She breaks the silence. "Two lovers who refuse to love one another for fear of a broken heart. How tedious. It bores me." Sibyl has little patience for love, those confessed or not.

Dao pitches forward at Sibyl's mischievous grin. "We did not come here for you to decipher what is happening between us," he counters, cheeks splashed with red. "We have told you what we know. Now, tell us what *you* know. What do we do from here?"

Sibyl trails her nail across the surface of the fate card. The cloudy mist within the card stirs at her touch. "The Choice-chosen, Hope-favored, and Fate-blessed's paths are now crossed. It is just as I predicted." *Though it was a harrowing journey,* she adds to herself.

"Yes, yes," he growls, thumping his fist against the table and startling Cyllian on the barrel where she squats. The table only comes with two chairs, and since she's so small, she insisted on taking it. "What do we do, crone?"

She flicks her gaze to them, annoyed at their very presence and stupidity. "Someone needs to orchestrate the Sutherland and Loess armies." She received word that morning from Emory of both pledges to aid the

Legion. It came as a shock to her, but she was happy to receive the parchment in Bastian's place. She had sent word to Sindray as soon as she had the chance.

He blinks at her, and Sibyl rolls her eyes once more. "Me?"

"Yes, you, you foolish man. Who else would I be talking to? The healer?"

"No." His answer is simple and clipped.

"You, Cyllian, Fawn, Kaymen . . . I couldn't think of anyone better than a historian, a healer, a shepherd, and a weapon's master forging the very material that'll change the face of this war. Together, you will shape the army for the coming days. You will shape what our Queen needs."

Dao flexes his jaw. Sibyl bets that a year ago, he would think it impossible. A month ago, he would have laughed if he were told he'd be in charge of so many soldiers. But she knows someone has to do it, and maybe, just maybe, if he can be part of freeing his people, he'll agree. If he knows what's good for him, anyway. She'll force the matter if she must.

"By ourselves?"

"Oh," Sibyl grins. "You will not be alone. By now, the Pirate Queen will have told Queen Seiba that she has the best spy of the realm. If he hasn't already told Luxlynn of our secrets, he will tell Queen Seiba to save his own life. We shouldn't expect anything but. She will know everything, and Luxlynn will tell the rest if only but to seat herself higher in her mother's eyes."

"Her mother's?" Cyllian asks. She wets her lips as realization finally dawns on her. "The Queen of Salix is Luxlynn's mother?"

Sibyl waves a hand in the air. "Old news, Shadow Woman. This is old news. But the one thing we can bet on is that she doesn't know about our allies. Not yet."

"And you couldn't have told us any of this before we knocked on Savage's door?" Dao demands. "You didn't foresee this?"

Sibyl's grin broadens to hide her shame. "Where would be the fun in that?" she lies, because in truth, she'd been focused only on one person: Nefari.

Shadow people are mixed with the centaurs and their living prisoners of war. At least, one hundred shadow people who are free and breathing, and . . . *free*. Nefari cannot believe it. She can't! All this time . . . Vale had told her, but she hadn't thought she'd truly witness it.

Nefari strides past them with wonder in her eyes as she heads to meet Bastian by crones' homes. "There are so many," she whispers in awe to herself. Some she recognizes, and others she doesn't, but they're alive. Breathing. *Living*.

271

Since this journey began, her world has turned. She hadn't realized how sheltered she was - how much Bastian had protected her from betrayals and secrets that were not his to divulge. She left Kadoka City as a child, and now, now she's a woman. A queen. A grasper of her own fate. And whatever may come, she'll take it.

Careful not to trip over ice chips, she whirls back to the task at hand. She'd deal with that revelation later.

Ahead, Bastian is talking with another, someone Nefari barely recognizes from her youth.

Shielding her eyes from the snow's bright glare, she calls, "Ostin?" Both men turn to her, and Nefari doesn't waste a second. She dashes, throwing her arms around this rugged and handsome man's neck, ignoring the blood on his cloak and leather vest.

"Princess," he answers, releasing her and bending a knee in the snow to show respect. He squints, surveys her, and then winks. "Or is it queen now?"

Nefari meets Bastian's gaze. She passes him a knowing look and straightens her shoulders as she proclaims, "Queen." She looks back to him and crosses her arms over her chest. "I thought you were all dead."

"I thought the same," Bastian grumbles under his breath. "Until the lot of them showed up in Kadoka City."

One of Ostin's bushy eyebrows raises. "Didn't Vale tell you otherwise? He's been traveling with you. Our watchers told us so."

"He told me some of the Guard survived, but I didn't believe him entirely. I didn't think there were so many," she adds, peering around them.

A grin plays at the edge of Bastian's lips. Pride fills his eyes. Pride that Nefari takes to heart.

Behind them, Vale, Beau, and Sindray approach. Nefari pays them no mind, continuing to grin at Ostin like a child having been gifted a toy. Bastian greets Vale with a shake of his hand, nods to Beau, and narrows his eyes at Sindray.

"And who are you?" Bastian inquires, an edge of defense in his tone.

"This is Sindray, the Choice-chosen," Nefari introduces.

"Friend or foe?"

Nefari holds up her hands to placate Ostin, whose hand immediately moved to his sword at the sight of the gentler crone. "Friend," she grinds out a bit because she's still sore about the whisperings. It is going to take her a while to come to terms with it.

"If you are the Choice-chosen, then where is your wolf?" Bastian asks at the same time Ostin looks to Vale and asks, "This is your informant?"

Sindray doesn't puff out her chest like Nefari would have, given the opportunity to show her strength. Instead, her posture remains the same, regal and graceful as always. "I do not command him. He travels by my side when he wishes."

Bastian relaxes but crosses his arms just the same. "And how did you tame such a beast?"

"He is not mine," Sindray counters with a grin. "He is the fee of the Dream Realm's wolf. A half to his soul, in fact, here to help guide me in matters of choice." She tips her head to the crowd of crones corralled by the centaurs. "What will you do with my people?"

"I assume you want to give them a choice," Nefari grumbles aloud.

"I do." Sindray nods.

Bastian's deep rumble sends a shiver over Nefari's skin. She knows the patronizing tone. "And that would be?"

"To follow me, of course."

"And if they don't?"

"Then you shall do with them what you will. I have killed enough today."

Bastian looks at her with a raised eyebrow. Nefari answers his wordless question with a wave of her hand. "She did it to save me, Vale, and Beau. And the crown, too." Vale holds up the bag with the crown as if called to do so. Their eyes land on it briefly.

"Beau," Ostin calls. "Why don't I show you to the others. I hear your sister lives in Kadoka City." With an arm around her shoulder, he leads her away and to a group of Onyx Guard men and women waiting not far away.

Conversation flows easily between Vale, Bastian, and Sindray after that, all of which Nefari ignores. She can't stop looking at the Onyx Guard – all of the free shadow people. All of the living souls she thought long dead. Vale hadn't lied to her. He told her the truth - that they still lived, and they showed up - for her. *For her.*

Wrenchel had been wrong. Perhaps - even though she hid away for years - perhaps they'd follow her and not blame her for being idle by hiding for a decade. Perhaps there was hope.

Nefari looks to the East where Kristal is surely being marched. *Hope.* She studies the trees as if she can see right through them to where Hope is being marched, right back into the hands of Despair. And Nefari let it happen. A bit of shame curls in her gut, and she presses a hand to it.

"If you'll excuse me, I have to send a message," Sindray excuses herself after a taut pause in the conversation about Kristal's whereabouts and the truth about who she is.

"To whom," Nefari inquires, pulled from her thoughts.

"To my cousin."

Bastian leans toward Vale as Sindray departs. "Who is her cousin?"

"Sibyl," Nefari answers for him, "Excuse me." Curious, she follows closely behind the gentle crone, and once they dip into the trees, Sindray says nothing about Nefari tagging along.

Instead, she says, peering up at the bone criers cawing above them, "Did you know you can send messages through the bone criers? Well, maybe not you, but the crones, if they remember the old ways. It isn't taught anymore."

Nefari breathes out the word, "No, I didn't know." When they come to a clearing with a small iced pond stretched out before them, the wolf joins them, trotting to Sindray's side. "Does he really belong to the fee of the Dream Realm?"

"He does," she answers then holds out her hand to the open air. A bone crier swoops and perches itself on her finger. She bends to the shore of the frozen pond, moves the tiny rocks around, and plucks out a black pebble.

Nefari watches her closely but inches away from the wolf whose maw is still bloody. She then eyes the large bird with suspicion. She's never seen one obey. She's never seen one do anything but caw at death and pick apart flesh.

"And you can really send messages with those things?"

Sindray nods and cups the stone. She brings it to her lips, whispers something Nefari cannot decipher, and then sets it on the pond, still holding the talons of the bird in the other hand. She moves until her face reflects against its glossy surface then blows breath across it. It fogs over, and once the fog disappears, she says to her reflection, "The battle is over, but the secret is no longer kept. The Queen of Salix will know she lives if she doesn't already, and Hope-favored is returning to her home. You must prepare for the Queen Seiba's wrath, cousin. The first place she'll look for the Fate-blessed is in the mountains." Sindray peeks a glance at Nefari then says to her reflection, "Be well."

She stands, dusts the snow from her dress, and plucks the stone from the ground. The bone crier holds up a talon, and she gives it the pebble. "Get this where it needs to go," she coos at the giant black bird. It takes flight and soars to the sky, heading west to the mountains far in the distance.

"That's it?" Nefari asks, breathless.

Sindray dusts her hand against the other. "Did you think it was some great magic?"

"Well . . . yes."

"It is nothing compared to what Wrenchel and the factions did with Salix."

Nefari cocks her head to the side and absentmindedly runs her fingers through the fur of the wolf. "What do you mean?"

She crosses the distance and bends to the wolf. She cups its jowls and the frozen blood among the fur there. "The crones cast a spell in the city's steel and iron.

"Like the cuffs?"

She nods without glancing at Nefari. "Like your cuffs. It weakens magic in Salix, which means anyone with magic who goes there will be weak."

"So if I travel there . . ." Nefari lets the sentence trail off.

Sindray finally looks at her. "Which means if you go there, you'll have little to no magic unless you can find a way to break dark Despair's magic."

"I have a way, I think, but I'm not sure how it'll work on the entire city."

Sindray raises to her feet. "Oh?"

"Inferaze. It's in the blade Kristal carries. And we have more." *If Dao was successful*, Nefari adds to herself.

"And this breaks Despair's magic?"

Nefari nods but doesn't go into detail when she adds, "I tested it myself."

"Then perhaps," Sindray thinks aloud but says nothing more. Her expression takes on a thoughtful look. "As for what Wrenchel said -"

Nefari holds up a hand. "I know what you're going to say."

"Do you?"

"Patrix was captured. And it serves him right, but like Vale, you're going to ask me to retrieve him."

"No." Sindray gives a small shake of her head. "For what he is destined for, you cannot save him. Not on his journey across Widow's Bay, nor in the castle of Salix's capital, Eveland. No. You will retrieve him the same way you'll save the Princess of Salix. You must find them when they're not inside the castle. When they're not by the queen."

"I have no plans of saving Kristal," Nefari whispers.

"But you must." She touches Nefari's elbow. "If you want to save your people, you will need all of the players of the coming games."

A war plays out in her head, teaming with her prophecy. It sends a dark shiver across Nefari's body.

"Darkness will yawn across the realm, but as the others told you, that does not mean what you think it does."

"Oh?" Nefari challenges with a sneer. "What does it mean? Because it sounds daunting to me."

Nefari backs up a step when, in Nefari's mother's voice, she says, "Darkness cannot dwell where there is light." She grips Nefari's shoulders. "You. You are light, Shadow Queen."

"Am I enough light?" she asks in a small voice, to which Sindray only grins.

"You won't be alone."

Nefari juts her chin. "How?"

"What Wrenchel did not tell you is that Patrix secured you allies before his capture."

"Oh?" Nefari's heart leaps with hope.

"There's a new Queen of Loess, the late queen's daughter," Sindray says. Nefari hadn't heard that the first queen died, and she doesn't have time to inquire about it.

Sindray continues, "And the young queen managed to convince her people and Sutherland to back the Queen of the Shadow Kingdom in the coming days." Nefari only blinks at the news, and Sindray shakes her. "Both land and sea allies, Nefari. You have an army. You will not be alone."

"And what of the crones?"

Sindray drops her hands. "I will see that the crones fall in line. There will be some who rebel. Not all were here today. Once the rebellion's dust has settled, we will come to Salix to ally with you. Urbana and Salix against the realm. It will be so."

Nefari looks at her ring, watching the stone reflect the snow that whirls about with the wind.

"The ring," Sindray comments. She takes her cold hand in her own. "Is this the same stone as that of the crown's?"

Nefari nods as she releases her hand. "It is inferaze."

"So that's why the crown did not work for Wrenchel. It had a piece missing."

"Two, actually."

Sindray laughs a great belly laugh. "Fate had an interesting way of securing your future, and at great cost to himself."

Nefari couldn't agree more. He must have foreseen the future, known the shadow people would need the inferaze to be freed. The crown had been passed through her family for generations, and the ring with it, at some point. To know the future of the shadow people was so grim, and to carry the weight of it for years to come . . . Nefari can't imagine what the knowledge must have done to him. Perhaps it is what stirred his action in the Realm's War, and now that war was on Nefari's doorstep, an unwelcome guest. It's in her prophecy, and she is to greet it. To embrace it.

"What will you do?" Sindray eventually asks. "What is your plan?"

"I'll take your advice, but Patrix knows everything," Nefari speaks truthfully. "He cannot stay within the Salix Castle walls. Not for long. Not without spilling his guts."

"Indeed. And to do anything about it, you need the Hope-favored."

"There you go again, talking about Kristal. I don't need her."

"In years of pain, the Hope-favored has been a silent witness to the darkness's violent reign. Both powerless and powerful, she will be the -"

"Hope to the captives who cower. I know." Nefari rolls her eyes.

"And on her eighteen birthday," Sindray continues with a cock of her eyebrow.

Nefari reluctantly looks her square in the eyes. "She will rise with the very shadows she befriends and become enemy to her own kin."

"Indeed," she says grimly. "She is already on her path to do so. What of you, Nefari? Will you let hatred stew? Or will you find forgiveness because your paths, all our paths, are now intertwined?"

It doesn't take long for Nefari to say, "I will do what I must to free my people and have my kingdom restored."

They look to the east together, to the wind that blows the falling snow. "Are you ready, Nefari Astra Galazee Ashcroft? Are you ready to face Despair's wrath?"

"I hope so."

The wolf raises his head and howls to the sky. A whole different sort of shiver crawls across Nefari's skin.

"Then, your fate has begun. Tomorrow, you, the Rebellion Legion, and the Onyx Guard will leave for Salix. Go. you must prepare yourself. Clean up that wound on your shoulder so you may cleave the darkness, Nefari."

On numb feet, Nefari turns and heads back to the way they came. She takes one step. Then another. And by the third, she raises the crown of shadows atop her head and whispers to the wind, "Queen."

We hope you have enjoyed The Reign of Silence (Heavy Lies the Crown). Please leave a review to help other readers who may enjoy this series as well. The next book's publishing date is projected for Fall 2021.

For series order, visit dfischerauthor.com.

Take a moment and follow D. Fischer on Instagram, Facebook, or Email. If you'd like to connect more exclusively, join her Facebook group, D. Fischer Reader's Group.

ALSO BY D. FISCHER

| THE CLOVEN PACK SERIES |

| RISE OF THE REALMS SERIES |

| HOWL FOR THE DAMNED |

| HEAVY LIES THE CROWN |

| NIGHT OF TERROR SERIES |

| GRIM FAIRYTALES COLLECTION |

ABOUT THE AUTHOR

Bestselling and award-winning author D. Fischer is a mother of two very busy boys, a wife to a wonderful husband, an owner of two sock-loving German shorthairs, and slave to a rescued cat. Together, they live in Orange City, Iowa.

When D. Fischer isn't chasing after her children, she spends her time typing like a madwoman while consuming vast amounts of caffeine. Known for the darker side of imagination, she enjoys freeing her creativity through worlds that don't exist, no matter how much we wish they did.

Follow D. Fischer on Facebook, Amazon, Bookbub, Goodreads, and Instagram.

DFISCHERAUTHOR.COM